PRAISE FOR STARLING

"A riveting story with an unlikely hero. Gina is the kind of woman who often goes unseen and is rarely the center of the narrative. Vensel White's novels offer no two-dimensional characters; all the people on the periphery have complicated stories and motivations. Like real life. You'll think about these authentic characters long after the story is done."

—Katie O'Rourke, author of *Blood & Water*

"Beautifully compelling and overflowing with artistic expression, a novel that captures the challenges and triumphs of the heart. Vensel White seamlessly forms a tapestry of prose with sharp yet lush descriptions and astute observations of the human dynamic. *Starling* shines light on the ways we imprison and ultimately release ourselves through the strength of our yearnings. A thoughtful and rich read that showcases the power of familial bonds."

—Cherie Kephart, award-winning author of *A Few Minor Adjustments*

Other Books by Mary Vensel White

The Qualities of Wood
Bellflower

STARLING

A NOVEL

Mary Vensel White

Winter Goose
PUBLISHING

Winter Goose Publishing
45 Lafayette Road #114
North Hampton, NH 03862

www.wintergoosepublishing.com
Contact Information: info@wintergoosepublishing.com

Starling

COPYRIGHT © 2022 by Mary Vensel White

First Edition, May 2022

Cover Design by Winter Goose Publishing

Paperback ISBN: 978-1-952909-15-3
Hardback ISBN: 978-1-952909-17-7

Published in the United States of America

For Diego, Satchel, Teagan and Geneva—my favorite stars

"In the desert
I saw a creature, naked, bestial,
Who, squatting upon the ground,
Held his heart in his hands,
And ate of it.

I said, "Is it good, friend?"
"It is bitter – bitter" he answered;
"But I like it
Because it is bitter,
And because it is my heart."

—Stephen Crane

Nest

1

Picture the start of a movie: Chicago in the rain. Streaked glass, water, towering metal. Crowded under bus stop shelters, people watch for the gleaming vehicles, moving through the storm like tanks. Where the streets build to a crest, the city is divided by its aortic river; the water's surface is chinked armor and foamy peaks, stitched by a series of steel bridges. The entire city glistens. Above the slick asphalt, brake lights surface like blurred pixels, this scattering of red in a gray, gray world.

The camera pans to a single office building. Rows of windows, stacked. A close-up of one...

Gina S. stands in Mr. Sheldon Seutter's half-lit office, watching the rain. She is middle-aged, of average build, with a gentle but plain face. Moments before, she'd been pacing and arranging, going about her normal office duties while a song from a Gap television commercial repeated in her mind.

Baby, baby, it looks like it's gonna hail. You gotta jump, jive, and then you wail. You gotta jump, jive, and then you wail.

The song is simple, mesmerizing, and it's been in her head all day. The visuals: dancers in t-shirts and khaki pants converge and split into various groupings. Three females join hands and synchronize feet, and then a boy lifts one onto his shoulders; her body is straight and lean as a yoke. The dancers are young and happy, perfect skin in various hues. And somehow this song, these gliding forms, are tied to a memory of Gina's father, talking about Elvis at a dinner party. He wasn't a music lover, at least to his family didn't appear to be, nor had he ever set foot in a Gap store. But this commercial and its joyful song bring Gina back, without apology or explanation, to that dense, summer evening when her father called Mr. Presley "fantastically musical." And to the look on her mother's face, a sudden glimmer of appreciation for her normally reserved husband. Both appeared to Gina in that moment, her lost parents, her mother's styled hair and beige, high-waist slacks, and his hands, pale and smooth, and the crevice between his eyebrows, that brief look exchanged; behind this single scene of memory, a huge vortex of flotsam swirled, an entire lifetime of what they had meant to her. Disappointments and protections. Their feel. Their scents. The times she had let them down and they, her. All because of a Gap television commercial.

As for time and place: a Friday afternoon, March of 1999. To an outsider looking into the corner office on the fourth floor of 17 LaSalle Street, it would appear that Gina attended to her usual business before pausing at the glass. Filing papers, settling items into their proper places. But as she watched the rain cover the city, her heartbeat accelerated.

"What can I do?" she mumbled.

Her coworker and friend, Nehra, had invited Gina to dinner on Saturday. She had also invited an acquaintance of her husband's, the latest effort in her quest to find Gina a mate. There had been two other men, two awkward lunches and one music festival. A year has passed since Nehra's last matchmaking effort and Gina had hoped she'd given up. Cohabitating people were naïve about the comforts of living alone, she often thought.

Gina watched the storm. Dark clouds filled the spaces between buildings like giant black splotches of paint. She checked her watch. The train to Berwyn ran every thirteen minutes but the later it became, especially on a Friday, the less chance she'd find a seat. But Mr. Seutter couldn't worry about her commute; his meetings were more important. She didn't mind. For almost twenty years, he'd been good to her.

"Gina?" Nehra leaned in, a purple scarf covering most of her hair. "Still waiting?"

"Yes." She walked past Nehra and out to her large cubicle. She pumped a dollop of hand lotion from a pink bottle then massaged it into her hands in a methodical way: palms, back of hands, each finger then the thumbs, individually.

"That smells like baby powder," Nehra said.

She shrugged.

Nehra had straight eyebrows accented with coal black pencil and she wore red lipstick, always. She lowered her voice. "Don't try to pull anything, Gina. Tom's been marinating the brisket."

Gina put the lotion back into a desk drawer. "With everything going on—"

"Yes, I know. You have to drive to the airport on Sunday. What does that have to do with Saturday night?"

She reached down and lifted her sneakers, a sock crumpled in each, from under the desk. Every Friday she changed the socks for a clean pair, another of her routines. She straightened up, slightly red-faced. "It's Ian," she said. "An important day."

"I would say so," Nehra said. "But Gina, you promised. Tom has that brisket, and I'm shopping the farmer's market in the morning."

Mr. Seutter's phone rang.

Nehra stood up, making her eyebrows into a stern V. "I'll pick you up at five, so you don't worry about driving."

The phone buzzed again. Nehra was already retreating.

Gina lifted the receiver and it slipped in her hand. "Good afternoon, Mr. Seutter's office."

"Is he gone already?"

She glanced at the clock. "Not back yet."

At the other end, Amanda Blevin exhaled loudly. "It's getting late."

Amanda Blevin—well-dressed, thin, perfumed, and jeweled. Gina sometimes felt like a piece of furniture next to her.

"I don't think I'll wait around," Amanda said. "Leave him a note for Monday, would you?"

"Sure." Gina reached for her pink message pad, glancing at her reflection in the computer screen. Plump face, brown hair split into two clumps of bangs.

"Wanted to share my thoughts on the meeting. I thought it went very well."

Mr. Seutter was working on opening a girls' charter school, and the meeting had been with potential supporters. Amanda was a star graduate from the public policy division Mr. Seutter endowed at the university, and now, his assistant. "And I wanted to get Mr. Dougall's contact information," she added.

"I have the yellow sheet here," Gina said. Whenever Mr. Seutter had a meeting, she typed one up with the attendees' phone numbers and addresses. She kept a copy and filed it afterwards. The new employee in charge of technology kept trying to get her to transfer her addresses to something on the computer. But her system had worked for years. Every night, she locked up her Rolodex in a filing cabinet and hid the only key. Heaven help them, she sometimes thought, if anything should happen to her.

"Never mind," Amanda said. "I'd better talk to him first."

"Well—"

"Gina, how long have you worked for him now?"

She stopped writing on her pad. "Over nineteen years."

Amanda chuckled. "You long-suffering girl."

"What do you mean?"

"It's a long time, right?"

"Mr. Seutter is a wonderful—"

"Oh, I know. I was just saying."

Gina set her pen down. She liked Amanda but sometimes it seemed they spoke different dialects of English, neither fully understanding the other, neither completely at ease in the other's company. When Amanda was hired, she was welcomed with an office-wide meeting. Mr. Seutter announced he was taking her under his wing, and he raved about her accomplishments in and out of school. Amanda had made certain efforts—she took the time to hear about Gina's filing system and method of keeping contacts—yet Gina couldn't get used to having her around.

Her thoughts returned to the weekend. Her brother, so far away. Ian and his wife Carrie were in Korea, meeting their new baby, and he'd asked Gina to pick them up at the airport on Sunday. How long had it been since she'd driven on the interstate? No matter. The baby's car seat was already strapped into her Saturn sedan.

The rain pelted the windows near Gina's desk, and she turned in her chair to look. Above nearby buildings, streaks of light pushed through the clouds. But the water blurred things, washing the screen of the window as it did.

She thought again of her parents, her mother's love of movies. Everyone knew Gina's sister had been named after the actress Deborah Kerr. Gina remembered a frequent sight: her mother, legs tucked underneath her on the tweed sofa, face lit by a flickering television screen. There was no getting her mother's attention if she was watching something.

Gina looked up from her desk. Mr. Seutter ambled down the long hallway, his coat dripping water from the hem. At eighty-three years old, he still walked two miles into the office most mornings. Mrs. Seutter, a second wife and fifteen years his junior, usually came in a bit later to oversee her charitable foundation. They'd drive home together in the evenings, or he'd call for a car if she'd already gone.

"Gina, you're still here." He paused at her desk. He was a tall man, over six feet, and still wore a suit well.

She shuffled through papers. "I have your telephone messages," she said, "unless you want to wait—"

"Let's look at those Monday." He took off his glasses and handed them to her. "Anything urgent?"

"No." She opened a drawer and found the cream-colored cloth. Carefully, she cleaned the rainwater from his spectacles.

He leaned against the wall. "I suppose I'll get the mail and be on my way."

"Everything's on your desk," she said.

"All right." He took the glasses from her outstretched hand. "Thank you, Gina."

At the end of each day for almost twenty years, Mr. Seutter had paused to thank her. He looked at her, truly saw her. Gina watched as he turned toward his office. His coat shimmered with droplets of rain.

She got her own coat from its hook and grabbed her umbrella. It took a few moments to lock things up, turn out lights, double-check that everything was in order. She stopped by Mr. Seutter's door. "Good night, then," she said.

He raised his head and in the soft glow from his desk lamp, he looked decades younger. Behind him, the city sparkled. "Good night," he said. "Stay safe getting home."

Once outside, Gina hurried along LaSalle Street, dwarfed by buildings on both sides. Three more turns and she'd be in the train station, then up the stairs to the platforms. She used to count the steps—ninety-four some days, ninety-six or seven on others; recently, she fought the urge. The rain fell clumsily now; the backs of her legs were damp. Two more turns and she'd be inside.

She entered the building and folded up her umbrella. The expansive lobby was bustling, the escalator filled to capacity. Once on the platform, Gina walked behind a young woman wearing green patent heels. So impractical for a rainy day.

I don't have time for fashion, her sister Deborah had complained when Gina visited her in Sacramento. Deborah's husband owned a carpet cleaning business and they had two sons. The ordinariness of her life was surprising, but before her marriage, Deborah had her share of adventure. In a box under her bed, Gina kept the postcards from Europe and Bermuda, from Australia and Hawaii.

During Gina's last visit—it must have been three years ago—the boys were booked with afterschool activities and the weekends weren't any less planned. There were neighborhood barbecues and endless errands, and Deborah had a few women's groups—Bunco, bingo, book club. She had volunteering commitments and PTA. Over the years, Gina's sister had hardened into a thinner, more resolute version of herself. But her hair remained blonde and styled into something current, and she still cared about Not Standing Out. This she retained from their mother.

Gina had tried to be helpful during her visit. She complemented the brick-enhanced house and the two boys who, despite certain defiant behaviors, seemed sincerely devoted to their mother. And if Deborah's hand shook a bit in the morning or she surreptitiously swallowed a little blue pill at lunchtime, well, none of that was Gina's business. They were both in their forties now; there were many things it could be.

As the train entered its mooring and squealed to a stop, Gina's thoughts returned to the dinner at Nehra's. "What can I do," she whispered, gripping her umbrella. Cautiously, she stepped up into the train. Inside, there were three seats left in the back section. She exhaled with relief as she sat down.

Gina settled in for the thirty-seven-minute ride home. As they left the city, the buildings spread out, and something also expanded in her. In this calmer, larger space, she thought about her brother, the man he had too quickly become.

Ian was tall like their father, with the same broad shoulders and curly, brown hair. In complexion and coloring, he took after their mother's side. He and Gina shared the pale, Nordic skin, and they both grappled with their weight. You need structure, she'd told him a million times, a schedule you can follow. Her haphazard brother.

During his childhood, Ian cycled through a variety of interests: a rock collection, baseball cards, Nigeria. One Halloween, he fashioned a costume from a chintz shirt, baggy pants, and a "fila" hat made with cardboard and fabric. Typical Nigerian dress, he claimed. He studied and prepared for weeks. After a heated talk with their mother, his teacher grudgingly gave him extra credit for the report he wrote about African history. Gina's mother believed in rewarding hard work, no matter what. Ian still had a tendency to dive headlong into things.

The train pulled into the Berwyn station with a sigh and a wheeze, like an old man rising from a recliner. Gina clutched her purse and scooted to the front of her seat. She loved her hometown, the broken-in feel of the streets and the parallel canopies of trees. Her father told them about the town's beginnings, about thousands of imported trees—maple, ash, cedar, poplar and pine—brought in by Thomas Baldwin and planted throughout the area, even before the railroad came in. And Gina had always wondered about the priorities of a man who put trees before a railroad.

When she emerged from the train, a light mist cooled her face, not enough for the effort of the umbrella. Her heart pounded in her chest. She tried not to look over her shoulder to see if anyone was following closely, because why would anyone want anything to do with her? The keys dug into the soft flesh of her palm. *Here's the one I want, next to the condo key, next to the tiny gold one for the safe. Sixty-five steps usually. Fifty-seven, fifty-eight, fifty-nine. Fifty-nine today. And open, and in.* New car smell, a faint trace of vanilla from the last time she'd taken it to the Nifty Wash on Oak Park Avenue. She locked the car, and the metallic thud instantly calmed her heartbeat.

This was Ian and Carrie's second attempt at adoption. The first had been right after their wedding. They'd completed paperwork, *oohed* and *aahed* over the photo of a blonde-haired baby boy, then the birth mother decided to give it another go. Ian and Carrie were heartbroken. One night while Ian was away on business, Gina brought soup over to their cold loft apartment and sat with Carrie. She knew her sister-in-law was suffering but couldn't muster much sympathy when they still had so many opportunities. Nothing was over for them.

And sure enough, within a year they were ready to try again, an international adoption. A little girl from Korea. Gina asked Carrie if that's where her people were from, and Ian became annoyed and told her Carrie was from Michigan. Gina thought he was being too sensitive. Maybe she didn't have the—what do they call it, political correctness—he'd learned in college, but it was a simple enough question.

The adoption process was a long one. Ian would telephone sometimes and tell her about the various aspects. The mountain of paperwork, the home study, the phone calls and waiting. Another photo arrived, a shock of black hair and deer-in-the-headlights eyes, a yellow bodysuit. And then it was time. They gave Gina the car seat and left in a flurry of last-minute instructions. Sunday at O'Hare, Ian said. Don't worry, they had everything they needed for the baby. Did they, though?

Guiding her car over the rain-cleansed streets of Berwyn, Gina took a deep breath. "Another day," she said. And the weekend stretched before her, palpable but indistinct.

2

Berwyn and Chicago, January 1968

Gina pinched the toast with two fingers and quickly transferred it to a plate. The toaster was old and unreliable, sometimes burning its contents to black, other times barely heating.

"Monmon," Ian said from his booster seat. "Monmon."

"Cinn-a-mon," she corrected. "I'm getting it now." She cut a sliver of butter from the stick and spread it on the toast, then sprinkled cinnamon on top.

"More!" Ian said. "Meema, more."

"There's no more left," she told him. "Look." She shook the cinnamon container upside down. Ian, at three, had no idea you could turn the lid to close off the holes.

He started on the toast with gusto, his chubby elbows extended. Pinkish cheeks, swirls of dark hair, his large, shining eyes.

"Eat your banana, too," she reminded him.

"You, Meema," he said, mouth full of sweet bread.

She patted his back on her way to the refrigerator. "I'm having grapefruit." In a plastic drawer, three grapefruits clustered in the corner. She chose the smallest one, planning to have a piece of toast with it. Just one, no butter.

At the table, Ian chugged milk from his cup as thin, white rivulets streamed down either side of his face.

The kitchen door swung open, and their father entered, dressed more for work than the weekend in pressed slacks and a button-up shirt. "Ready for our adventure?"

"Mommy," Ian said, looking back and forth between them.

Gina reached over to wipe the dribble of butter from his chin. "She's with Auntie Klara in Atlanta, remember? She'll be home tomorrow."

Henry placed his coffee mug on the table. "And we're having an excursion today. You're going to be a good boy, aren't you?"

Ian nodded, squeezed the banana until it oozed a bit between his fingers.

Deborah walked in, smelling of Love's Baby Soft, powdery and fresh. Her hair was pinned back on one side with a jeweled barrette. She had just turned fifteen and for nine weeks, could brag two years' seniority until Gina turned fourteen.

"ETD is nine thirty," their father said, pouring coffee into his mug.

"What's that?" Gina asked.

"Estimated time of departure."

"Dork," Deborah said to Gina.

He turned in the doorway on his way out. "Girls, a reminder. We have a three-year-old boy to keep track of today. Thousands of people will be milling around the city, and the last thing I want to worry about is you having one of your arguments while Ian is whisked away by some stranger."

Deborah snickered. "Who would want him?"

They looked at Ian, who had converted his banana into a mound of yellow Playdoh.

"Yes, well, they won't know his habits when they first see him."

Deborah poured herself a bowl of Frosted Flakes. Not fair, Gina thought for the hundredth, maybe thousandth time. Her sister's narrow waist and shapely legs, while she was stuck with thick tree stumps.

"Great," Deborah said. "The last day before Mom gets home and we're stuck going to a museum."

Gina shrugged. "He said we can get hot dogs in the park."

"How exciting." Deborah shoved a heaping spoonful into her mouth. "Let's get one thing clear," she said between chews. "You're in charge of *It*."

She pointed her thumb at Ian and something about the entire scene, Deborah's full mouth or the way she leaned, simian-like, over the table, the look of disgust on Gina's face, or maybe even just the thumb and the fact that their eyes simultaneously followed its direction, something about it made a chunk of mutilated banana fly from Ian's mouth, followed by a gusty laugh. That monotonous, hilarious baby laugh of his, until his sisters joined in, and they all laughed around the table.

They took their father's car, the Ford. ("I'm not driving that thing," he had said about their mother's station wagon.) They cleared the trash and crumbs, the magazines and half-read newspaper sections, onto the floor where they stomped it down with their wet boots. Wet because the lawn was still covered in a sleek layer of snow, which they had jumped around in before getting into the car. Something their mother would have never allowed.

"Bye-bye," Ian called from the back seat, where he stood next to Gina. Deborah got the front seat, of course, being the oldest.

They watched as the brick brownstone faded through the back window, rapidly blending into the row of houses. Ian continued to wave. "Bye-bye, bye-bye!" Gina waited for him to sit down and buckled the seat belt around his belly. Their mother always insisted on seatbelts, even though hardly anyone used them.

"We're on Harlem Avenue," Henry announced when they had cleared the neighborhood and turned onto a wider road. "Can anyone guess where 'Harlem' comes from?"

"What do you mean?" Deborah asked.

"The name," he said. "Harlem." His eyes found Gina's in the rear-view mirror, and she looked away.

"New York?" Deborah said, popping her gum.

"Yes, but no." He stopped at a red light and turned around. "Any guess?"

"Nope," Gina answered.

"It's a Dutch name. You know this area was settled by Dutch, Czechs, Swedes like your mother."

"What about your family?" Gina asked.

"Yes. Yugoslavians, Poles, Italians. A real hodge-podge. That great-great-great English grandfather who gave us our surname." He turned into the flow of traffic on the interstate. "An early investor by the name of Thomas Baldwin bought the first 347 acres of land and he imported thousands of trees. One of the first things he did…"

Gina stared out the window, letting her father's deep voice blend into the street noise of cars and wind. She wondered what her mother was doing at Aunt Klara's that very moment, so far away but still part of the same day, under the same hazy sun. She waited for a break in her father's lecture and asked, "Why did Aunt Klara need surgery?"

He sighed, annoyed at the sudden change of topic. He looked at Deborah, who gave back a faint glare, a look of exasperation, something they shared at Gina's expense. "It's a surgery that women have sometimes," he said.

"Red car!" Ian chirped.

"What do you mean?"

"Gina, it's probably somewhat personal."

"Geez," Deborah said, shaking her head.

"Sorry for caring." Gina reached up and traced a pattern of circles on the fogged window.

"She'll be fine, if that's what you're wondering." Her father reached over and turned on the radio. "She won't have any more children, that's all."

"Meema, get out."

"Not yet," she told Ian. "Look at all the cars."

He whined and slammed his head into the vinyl seat. "Get out now."

She reached into her purse and found the bag of dry cereal she had packed for him. At the sight of it, he sat up and extended a pudgy hand.

The longest part of the trip was maneuvering through downtown. On Saturdays, the streets were packed with tourists and day-trippers like themselves. Silently, they took in the sights: outside downtown, the billboards and cars whizzing by, then the giant skyscrapers and bundled pedestrians, people gathered at every street corner and streaming along the sidewalks on either side. They drove underneath an L platform and Ian strained his neck watching the noisy train pass overhead.

"Michigan Avenue," her father announced. On this busy street, tall buildings lined one side like well-dressed gentlemen, and the feminine curves and expanse of Grant Park graced the other.

Gina remembered the park from two other trips with her father. Walking through flower gardens, a path that wended along railroad tracks, the majestic stone fountain spraying loops of water. Her mother didn't like the city, but she came down occasionally for shopping or a special dinner with friends. Hard to believe it was less than fifteen miles away, Gina thought, as different as it was from Berwyn.

Henry parked on the street. "Bring your coats," he said. "Gina, hold onto Ian at all times."

They walked a couple of blocks, trailing behind their father and his long-legged strides, until they gathered at the base of a wide, cement staircase. On either side, two statues framed the entrance: green lions standing guard with their mouths open and teeth bared. Arches were cut into the facade of the building, high above the grand entrance, and colored banners hung in each one.

"Let's go." Her father carried Ian up the stairs. In the lobby, he bought tickets and they left their coats.

In the first room, canvases hung along the length of a wall, all equidistant between the ceiling and floor, all roughly the same size and split into two spheres by a horizon. Many were scenes with water and sky, the imprecise line of the horizon at varying heights but always water below and a soft dissolve into the sky above. Gina found herself staring at one in particular, streaks of color across the canvas, brown and yellow changing to a strip of blue, lightening to yellow again with blue seeping through. Land, water, cloudy sky. Near the bottom, a dark figure stood, legs together as though a single post, arms tucked into a short coat, head mostly an outline against the vivid bands. You couldn't even be sure it was a person, but Gina knew how he felt.

Her father and Deborah walked along, talking, and reading the placards beside each painting. As though nobody else existed in the world. Gina turned to the painting on her right, a greenish-blue variation of sea and sky, then looked at the next one, which was grayer in tone. Both were titled Nocturne something. She thought about catching up to her father and asking what it meant, but before that idea had fully formed, a piercing yell cut through the silence.

Ian. Aghast, she looked down at her hand, to which he was no longer attached. How and when she had let go, she couldn't say. Turning round and round, she scanned the room. She hurried around a corner and into a smaller room full of portraits but no little boy.

Gina turned as another squeal echoed. *The hallway.* Briskly, she entered the vast corridor. There were several entryways she hadn't noticed on the way in. Each seemed to lead to another small room like the one she'd just been in. Some rooms were joined to others by narrow walkways at the back. She entered one and took the passage to another, following the occasional sound of Ian's voice.

"Red!" she heard him say once. "Red ball!" A few moments later, as she jogged through another room, she heard the beginning of the ABC song, referenced by his three-year-old brain whenever he saw writing of any sort.

She went back to the hallway, stood for a moment straining her ears, looking at the row of entryways that were like a cartoon, when the characters chase each other in and out, always missing by moments. Then Ian's head appeared from one, the glistening eyes, the springs of dark hair. "Meema!" he said and with a delighted giggle, disappeared again.

Her father and Deborah arrived from another portal, his face a strange color, her mouth closed for once. "Where's Ian?" he asked.

She pointed to the room, and they hurried over. At the entrance, they stood and looked in.

Throughout the space hung an array of black-and-white photographs, all city buildings and streets. Some were grainy and others were sharply focused. But it was Ian who captured and kept their attention, because he was like a wild thing, running circles around the room, his little feet tap-tap-tapping on the tile, squeaking when he turned to run back the other way. His voice was full of exclamations and now that he'd spotted them, insistences.

"Wook! A fire, a fire. Wook, Meema!"

He pointed to a photograph of a bridge, great heights, and lengths of steel, then darted across the room, bouncing from one photo to the next, as though he'd lost control of his senses.

"Lights, so tall. So tall."

He held his hands up, thumbs bent so that each hand formed an L, framing the photograph in front of him now: ticker tape falling over an urban landscape.

"Ian!" their father said.

Everyone seemed to snap out of something, return to themselves.

Henry strode across the room, his long legs like exclamation points against the white of the tile. He scooped up Ian and held him against his chest. When he reached the opening to the room, where the sisters remained shoulder-to-shoulder and motionless, he leaned over and whispered savagely. "I asked you to do one thing, Gina."

It took a while for the toddler to calm down. They found a bench where they could sit for a while. Ian was in an excitable state and when he realized no one would share his buoyant mood, he started to whine and struggle to break free. Gina distracted him with more of the dry cereal.

They continued on, touring the museum. They had a nice lunch in the park, hot dogs as Henry had promised. Ian ran around again, unfettered amidst the trees, his breath trailing after him in puffs. Further up Michigan, they parked near the historic Water Tower and their father told them about the first city, built back up after the fire. He focused his attention on Gina, trying to make amends, and asked Deborah to keep track of Ian in the bird-filled courtyard, where people milled around and once, a gap-toothed man held a hat towards Gina. They sat on a bench, watching the city life swirl around them.

In that moment, with her nose red from cold and the gray day throbbing around her, with the birds pecking and jumping, and the sting from the incident at the museum losing its edge, Gina knew what she'd remember most about the day: her brother's capacity for joy. And just as that thought occurred to her, Ian escaped from Deborah's clutches. He ran around the courtyard as Deborah chased him, eventually clinging to Gina's legs, his mischievous face peering up from between her knees. And before long, they were all laughing again.

3

"There you are, Gina! I've been waiting on you, must be forty-five minutes now."

Gina looked across the yard, countless blades of grass gleaming with rain. Mrs. Spark stood on her porch, backlit by the light, surrounded by her collection of garden figurines.

"You fixed the leprechaun," Gina said.

"In time for Saint Paddy's." The old woman beckoned with her bony fingers. "Here, here. Come out of the rain."

Gina glanced at her own clutter-free porch next door. She didn't bother to mention that the rain had stopped. "Thank you, Mrs. Spark," she said, stepping up.

There was hardly room to stand amongst everything: seven dwarves with their familiar faces, a plastic Virgin Mary with a faded mantle, three wire deer strung with lights, a blow-up figure of Pop-Eye, a gray stone rabbit and his friend, the stone squirrel, a bat with orange lights tacked to the banister and in the corner of the porch, a crèche complete with animals, shepherds, and wise men. There was a story Gina had heard many times, which explained why Mrs. Spark had two black wise men. Mrs. Spark felt she had to explain this every so often to avoid someone getting the wrong idea.

Mrs. Spark leaned forward, squinting. She was small and compact, crackling with energy. Grayish hair, usually covered with a red headscarf, dark sweatpants with enough room for another person, tee-shirts with slogans like *I Found Puget Sound* or *Hostess is Best*. None of it with any relation to Mrs. Spark. Gina knew her neighbor bought most of her clothing at the local Goodwill because this was another favorite topic, along with the end of the world and her ungrateful son. These last two seemed related in the old woman's mind.

"Someone was looking for you," Mrs. Spark said.

"What do you mean, here?" Gina glanced again at the entrance to her condo. Aside from package deliveries or the occasional visit from Ian, she didn't get much company.

"A woman."

"What woman?"

Mrs. Spark crossed her arms and stared straight ahead. With the red scarf and her longish nose, she looked like a gypsy from an old movie.

"You saw a woman?" Gina prompted.

"Oh, yes." She touched Gina's arm. "She's a nurse. What's wrong with you?"

"Nothing. Did she say what she wanted?"

The old woman tilted her head. "She knocked on my door and asked if that was your place."

"What did you say?"

"What should I say? She wasn't the mafia." She cocked an eyebrow. "Do you owe someone money?"

"No, no." Gina said. "I'm sure it was some sort of salesperson." She stepped down to the lower step. "I guess I'll get myself some dinner."

"You'll be around this weekend?"

"Not much," she said. "I've got a dinner tomorrow and Sunday is the airport."

Mrs. Spark clapped her gnarled hands. "Oh, my goodness! Won't you bring the baby over?"

"Oh, Mrs. Spark. It's not my—I mean, I'm sure they'll be wanting to get home."

"Of course, yes." She looked away.

Gina thought of Mrs. Spark's ungrateful son and the few times she'd seen him, driving up without his family, hurrying back to the car with his head down. Mrs. Spark believed the estrangement had been caused when she accidentally insulted the daughter-in-law's cooking one Thanksgiving; Gina thought there was probably much more to the story. Still, she blamed the son for not clearing the air. Mrs. Spark was an old woman. There was little time remaining for pride and there'd be much more later for regret.

"I'll be here tomorrow morning," she offered.

But Mrs. Spark had turned away, already had a hand on her doorknob.

"Good night," Gina said. She walked over to her porch, the simple yellow glow of the porch light, the wooden planks needing paint, and it wasn't until she had her key extended that she realized Mrs. Spark had followed her, was calling her back.

"She left this for you." In the old woman's hand, a small paper, a business card.

Gina thanked her and shoved it into her coat pocket. Mrs. Spark disappeared around the corner and quickly scaled the steps to her porch, still miffed about not seeing the baby. She could be surprisingly agile at times.

One satisfying click, one smooth turn, and Gina was up, over the threshold, into the living room. Door closed; bolt extended.

Gina completed a checklist whenever she arrived home. First, she brushed the moisture from the shoulders of her coat before hanging it carefully on the same, silver hanger. She unlaced her sneakers and aligned them on the rubber mat in the closet, with the shoelaces tucked inside. In her bedroom, she put on her slippers, a Christmas gift from her brother. Blue with fleece lining, a small satin bow over the toes. The type of present you buy someone when you run out of ideas. Back in the living room, she turned the television to the nightly news. And when everything was in its place, Gina went to the kitchen cabinet where she kept her small bottles of spirits. Once she had finished half the glass and could feel its warm balm, only then did she walk back to the closet and reach into the deep pocket for the business card.

Sandra Pierce, R.N.
Allshare Medical Group – Berwyn

A salesperson after all, she thought, ignoring a creeping, unsettled feeling. She'd never been to a place called Allshare, had never heard that name, had she? With a tiny, clapping sound, she set the card on the counter.

She chose her dinner from the freezer. Swedish meatballs, string green beans on the side. Three minutes in the microwave, stir the noodles, another minute and a half. She used to cook more. She'd had her specialties, recipes inherited from her mother: spaghetti, meatloaf, tuna casserole. She used to make big batches then split them in half, sometimes freezing the second portion for a Wednesday dinner with Ian, sometimes having it the next weekend herself. Lately, she'd lost interest.

The beeping of the microwave startled her and for some reason, at that exact moment, she glanced at the telephone answering machine. The small black display was illuminated with a red, blinking number two.

She retrieved her dinner and pulled back the plastic cover. The steam washed over her face. She took the food and her glass to the dining room table and ate slowly.

Ian had been an adorable child, not skinny but to Gina's mind, perfectly within the realm of healthy. Aunt Klara called him "Pitepalt," which always seemed to bother Gina's mother as much as when she called her Helena instead of Helen. When or why her mother had dropped the "a" from her name, Gina never knew. She did, however, ask Aunt Klara once about the meaning of Pitepalt: a Swedish dumpling, usually pork. Gina's aunt lived in Atlanta, so they didn't see her often.

In high school, Ian grew taller and heavier. At first it didn't seem to bother him but by the time he entered the University of Illinois in 1983, he was constantly trying to lose weight. Protein powders, liquid diets, salads, and whole grains, and still, Gina would find empty wrappers in his room: Doritos, O'Henrys, hot dogs from 7-11.

Once he tried a protein-only diet, which he explained to their mother over a Wednesday dinner after refusing the potatoes and rolls she had prepared.

"Atkins, Mother," he said patiently. "Not Perkins."

Helen pointed her fork at him, her lips creating a radius of deep lines above her mouth. "Explain to me again," she said, "how this diet works."

Gina was in her late thirties then, still living in the nearby brownstone she rented the second time she moved out. This would have made her mother about sixty-five, a few years before she passed. Gina always walked the ten minutes from her place for the Wednesday dinners or whenever she came over. Helen was slowing down and needed help with cleaning, lifting things and sometimes, with remembering. She was aging too quickly, but this was not a tangible thought Gina had; it surfaced as a general worry when she saw her mother gingerly step down from a stool or rub her arm, wincing. Whether any of these signs should have been a warning, a preparation for the illness to come, Gina didn't know. But they did not warn, did not prepare at all.

That night, they were all in good spirits. Ian was renting the upper floor of a brownstone on Oakdale, a five-minute walk in the opposite direction of Gina's. They met up quite a bit for lunches on the weekends, sometimes even a movie or a trip into the city for a Bears game.

"Your body spends a lot of energy burning carbohydrates," Ian explained.

A warm evening, humidity seeping into the house like fog, eluding the whir of the fan. Ian's face was slick with perspiration; two half-circles widened under the arms of his white tee-shirt.

Helen waved her dinner roll. "Like bread?"

He nodded. "Yes. Pasta, starches, things like that. You eliminate those, also sugar and anything that turns to sugar."

A raised eyebrow from Helen at this, but no comment.

He put his hands behind his head. "What you're doing is changing your whole metabolism. Your body starts to use its energy against the fat."

"Makes sense to me," Gina offered.

"Your body attacks the fat? What does that mean?" Helen closed her mouth tightly.

"Your body breaks down what you eat," Ian said. "So, it's always working."

Turning her roll this way and that, their mother took another bite. "I think I'd rather be fat than give up bread."

Ian's arms came down; he leaned forward. "You're lucky, Mom. You don't have to worry about it."

"We *all* have to worry about it, Ian," she said in a low voice. "It's—"

"What can you eat?" Gina interrupted.

"That's one of the misperceptions about Atkins," Ian said. "You can eat almost everything in small amounts, but mostly you eat vegetables and meat."

"I've never seen you eat vegetables." Gina recalled many dinnertime scenes, Ian stuffing green beans into his socks and once, lining up asparagus on the wooden ridge underneath the table.

"I'm trying." He smiled his winning smile. "But I do like meat, and I can eat as much as I want."

Forks clinked for a few moments as they finished their meatloaf, and Ian passed the bottle of white wine. "Steak, hamburgers," he said. "Chicken, pork chops, ribs, bacon, even fish, any kind of fish. All of it, every meal if I want."

Helen leaned back in her chair, crossing her arms over the lilac blouse with the pearl buttons, the one she used to wear on holidays but now brought out sometimes for Wednesday dinners. And she said, famously, "No offense, sweetheart, but you're not a lion."

They laughed immediately, and her face lit with surprise and pleasure. Her own laughter spurted up, geyser-like, while her face reddened and became youthful, and they continued like that for several minutes.

Strange, that Gina and Ian always remembered this, although it was uncharacteristic of their mother in so many ways. Helen never used the word "sweetheart," and she wasn't quick-witted or sarcastic. Over the years, how many times had they recalled this scene, their mother's surprising line, whenever diets were mentioned, or weight gain, or weight loss, and this became part of their conception of her and how things were during that period, when they all lived close together.

The Atkins diet didn't work. Ian remained husky and Gina couldn't help but think that if he walked more or tried to contain himself, his endless enthusiasm, maybe he could become thinner. Self-control, a routine—these were foreign to Ian's nature.

Gina rinsed the last traces of her dinner down the sink and turned to face the answering machine. Her glass was empty. She walked over and pushed the gray button.

Beep.

Friday, March 12th. Two new messages.

Beep.

Four forty-three p.m.

Gina, it's Ian. (Traffic in the background). *You're probably on your way home.*

Gina's heart clenched. Ian, calling from Korea.

Everything is fine, but I wanted to talk to you. (Here, his voice became slightly clearer, as though he had cupped his hand over the receiver.) *Gina, we saw the baby. We saw Hana. She's great, everything is great, but I need— Listen, I'll call you later. Don't worry.*

Beep.

Six fifteen, p.m.

Gina looked at the kitchen clock. Seven twenty-four.

Hello, uh, Gina, this is Sandra Pierce. This is my fourth message and I tell you, I'm not exactly sure why you're not returning my calls. You know, I want to get these papers to you, these records, and I'm trying to do the right thing, because they're confidential. They could have ended up God-knows-where, after Dr. Trainor passed and what, with no one taking responsibility. I've got boxes in my apartment, all these records and you know, most people are glad to have them. Took me a while to find your address, so that was my time spent, too.

Gina, frozen to the spot, began to rub her arms.

I spoke to your neighbor. I was going to leave the packet on your porch but wasn't sure about that. After I left, I realized I should have put it in your mailbox. Anyway, Gina, that's what I'm going to do tomorrow. I'll come by and drop them in the mailbox. Because there's no one else to do this, Gina. Really, I'm trying to be nice. Well, good-bye.

Beep.

End of messages.

Beep.

Gina walked to the cupboard, reached for another mini bottle of Snow Leopard vodka. Her last one. She never knew what they would have in stock at the local liquor store; their supply of mini bottles was always changing. Sometimes, the cashier advised her to get the bigger bottle, but Gina liked having variety (although she chose mostly vodkas) and limits. If you only opened one bottle, there was no chance of over-indulging. No one could say anything about one tiny bottle.

She had purchased ten of the Snow Leopards. She loved the icy white design, the sulking leopard across the bottom of the bottle. Many of the vodka bottles made her think of chilly, pristine places. Snow Leopard was from Poland, she had noticed, and this fact even made her feel cosmopolitan.

More club soda, a squeeze of lemon, and her brain jolted back to Ian's call. She knew her brother, knew the inflections of his voice and how he sounded trying to be brave. At least she knew he wasn't hurt because she would have been able to tell. It had to be something with the baby, the adoption. Hana. She couldn't get used to that name, couldn't get used to her baby brother with a baby of his own, especially an Asian baby—she didn't care, no one could hear her think this—and she was trying to be politically correct, trying to be cosmopolitan but there it was, that thought. It wasn't the way she thought it would be. Deborah's boys were exactly what she might have imagined—blonde, tall, unabashedly confident. Just like Deborah. But Ian, her Ian. He was supposed to have a round, little baby with dark curls, a boy with the same dimples and sweet demeanor.

Gina took another long drink, imagining Poland. Snow drifts, sleek leopards, Julie Christie's fuzzy, white hat in *Doctor Zhivago*. She actually *was* cosmopolitan enough to know the movie took place in Russia but assumed the two places were very similar. Suddenly, like a snow leopard tiptoeing onto the scene, it came to her: Sandra Pierce, the nurse who used to work for Dr. Trainor. Doctor Raymond Trainor, a Northern Illinois student at the same time as Gina's father, before Trainor transferred to Urbana-Champaign for pre-med. Their family doctor until she moved out the second time, after she felt Ian could protect himself from Helen's dependency, in fact, after Ian himself had moved out, post-college, to start work and life. And Gina had an issue with her dentist and needed to confirm something with a primary care doctor. She hadn't had a physical for years and couldn't see Dr. Trainor, so she chose a new doctor from the list provided by her insurance company. She started to have semi-regular physicals at Dr. Tam's office downtown, instead of the converted brownstone where Dr. Trainor saw patients in Berwyn. And she never finished things up with Dr. Trainor's office, never had her medical records forwarded, and now, twenty years later—

Ian. So far away, and she had missed his call because she took a later train. Gina finished her drink and walked to the living room, the blue slippers dragging a bit. She stopped at the cabinet where she kept her VHS tapes of mostly older movies and her growing pile of *Redbook* magazines. Next to those, a small stack of spiral notebooks. She took one from the top, a green notebook, and sat down to write a letter, which always seemed to refocus her. A letter to her daughter in California. She would fill it with all the things she did during the week, maybe add a few to make it more interesting. She'd inquire about Michelle's job as a schoolteacher. Michelle, her daughter. Did that student, the one with derelict parents, did he pass his history exam? What ever happened with the situation in your apartment building, the violinist who was practicing late in the evening? How is the weather this time of year? Michelle, her distant daughter, whom nobody knew about except, strangely enough, her neighbor Mrs. Spark.

4

Berwyn, June 1976

Ian stood near the window. He was a chubby boy with brown, curly hair, wearing his mother's yellow housedress over plaid pajama pants.

The kitchen was the cheeriest part of the house. There were white curtains patterned with tiny blue gondolas, a new dishwasher, and clean, pale blue linoleum. The cabinets had been updated with dark iron knobs. Weekly, Gina's mother pulled out the shiny refrigerator and swept the debris behind it. She kept the windows smudge-free, the sills pristine.

Gina opened the refrigerator and found the pitcher of Kool-Aid. "Let me guess," she said. "You're a Nigerian."

Ian's face lit up. "How did you know?"

"That's all you talk about," she said.

"I made the costume myself."

"Costume?"

"Duh," he said. "For Halloween."

"That's months away." Gina glanced at the door. "Have you told Dad?"

"Why?"

"No reason."

In thirty minutes, Gina needed to leave the house without raising suspicion. She couldn't say she was going to the movies again; she'd used that excuse earlier in the week. She didn't bother to rationalize why she felt compelled to hide her relationship from her parents. After all, she was twenty-two years old. No one thought to ask Deborah what *she* did with her time. Everyone was accustomed to Deborah having boyfriends.

Gina hadn't had much experience in high school or afterwards. A few dates and one, month-long relationship. But she was still young; in fact, she felt quite optimistic about life since landing her first job straight out of secretarial school. Her parents hadn't been pleased when she quit community college, but they must be satisfied with her state of employment. They didn't seem to be in any rush for her to move out of the house—at least, they never mentioned it. In many ways they were accommodating but no, Gina didn't think they'd understand why she was dating one of the brokers from work, a man several years older and in the process of leaving his wife.

"Gina," Ian said.

She paused in the doorway. "What?"

"I like your shirt. Did you buy it with your insurance money?"

"My money from the insurance company job, you mean?"

"Yeah."

Gina looked at her watch. She'd still have time for makeup and hair if she started in ten minutes. "I like your costume too," she told Ian. "What's it called?"

His face spread into a grin. "A buba. That's the shirt."

"Buba," she repeated.

"The pants are called sokoto." He stood to show her. "I don't have a fila. That's a cap."

"What about the fighting? Do they have a uniform for fighting?"

"Probably," he said, "but since General Muhammed got assassinated, it's been relatively peaceful."

Relatively peaceful? What kind of eleven-year-old said things like that? As she often did, Gina worried about Ian fitting in. Unlike everyone else in the family, he was a genuine, no-holds-barred extrovert. Coming as he did, eleven years after his sisters, with no younger siblings and the only boy to boot—it was an unlucky situation for a talkative child.

"They're making states," Ian told her. "They'll have a new capital."

"That's great," she said. And for the next several minutes, she let him tell her about Nigeria, his current interest. Before that it was dentistry and before that, hydroplanes.

She'd never been able to resist her little brother. His cheeks folded into two long dimples when he smiled, and his eyes were brown but never dull. Flecked with gold and green, they were his single, best feature. Recently, he'd started wearing glasses, as Gina had at his age. Deborah had escaped the faulty genes. She never had to worry about her vision or her weight, or about getting sunburned, having inherited the darker coloring and trim physique of their father. The savory side of the family, their mother would say without emotion.

The Sahlins, her mother's family, had been in Berwyn for generations, part of the original influx of Swedes who settled along 31st Street in an area quickly dubbed "Swedetown." They were fair and blonde-to-brown. Gina remembered walking to a local bakery with her grandmother for biskvi cookies—lemon for her grandmother and always chocolate for Gina—and listening to the musical, choppy conversations of the women who would come to visit and drink kaffe. Grandma Sahlin spoke broken English but always had a long hug for Gina, and for her mother, advice delivered over steaming mugs at her kitchen table. Now and then the conversation punctuated with "English, Mother. Please." Gina's mother resisted Swedish, claiming she could no longer make sense of it.

Grandma Sahlin had known Ian only as a baby and for babies, she'd had little patience. Gina always thought it a shame Ian didn't get to know her, never had sweet biskvi cookies and grapefruit juice stirred with sugar. A stroke took her in 1967, when Gina was thirteen. Gina's mother once called it a blessing, claiming if Grandma Sahlin had lived through the cultural turmoil of 1968, she surely would've had a heart attack. Gina remembered only fragments and impressions of her grandmother: the smell of the quilt in the guest room and its pattern of stars and tiny green leaves, Grandpa Sahlin's engraved sword hanging over the mantle, her mother's deep sobs at the funeral. When Ian asked about their grandmother, Gina told him about the quilt and the sword, the cookies and the women who came to visit, and she felt guilty for not remembering more.

A bitter shame, as people say, the fact that Grandma Sahlin never really knew Ian. Gina's grandmother and the impressions she had left, like grooves on a record, and her brother, the center of so much. It didn't seem possible their orbits had barely crossed.

As Ian continued his discourse on Nigeria and its politics, Gina listened politely, for selfish reasons. She felt a constant pull where her brother was concerned and after letting him speak, she'd be able to leave the house guilt-free.

The broker was a nice man with clean, soft hands and a reliable Plymouth, and he made regular efforts to flatter her. They met at a pub or infrequently, at Benny's Bistro, where he always picked up the bill. Like Gina, he lived in Berwyn and rode the train into the office downtown. They noticed each other because of this, and it wasn't until much later, when the thing had fizzled out and the broker started avoiding her glances in the lunchroom, that she realized the shared commuter path was the only thing they really had in common. The relationship was reliable and easy while it lasted but Gina was often unbalanced in his presence, not knowing what to do or how to do it. An actor playing a part. Here, the line about the mild weather, there, a hand grasped under the table.

This night, they had a quiet dinner at Benny's, then sat in his car for a while. When Gina returned from the date with fresh lipstick and a wrinkled blouse, her parents were in the kitchen with the door closed. She paused at the foot of the stairs to listen.

"I don't understand it," her father was saying.

"What's to understand?" her mother said. "He has interests. You of all people should understand that, with your face in a book most of the time. A phone call from Deborah once a month practically. Everyone around here with their interests and their fascinating lives."

"We're talking about Ian."

"Yes."

"You find nothing strange about a fifth-grade boy going to school in black face?"

A muffled but aggressive laugh from her mother.

"Helen."

"Sorry, dear. You look so exasperated."

"I still have the ability to amuse you," he said. "That's something."

"He's a boy," her mother said. "He has a vivid imagination and no one to play with."

"This neighborhood is full of children."

"No, Henry. The neighborhood was full of children ten years ago. Deborah is twenty-three. All her friends have moved. She's gone."

"Helen, if you don't take care—"

"If *I* don't take care?" Angry sounds of dishes settled on the counter. "What should I be doing?"

"I know it's different with a boy."

"Do you?"

"I go to work every day, Helen. Would you like to pack your lunch tomorrow, ride down to my office and deal with—"

"And now there's the job."

This was a common topic, her father's job and how it prevented him from so much. And her mother's resentment of the job, nothing new, almost as if she were jealous. Gina shifted on her feet. They wouldn't start *that* this late.

A short silence then her father, cooling. "He can't be an African for Halloween, that's all. I am putting my foot down."

More dishes clattering in the sink, a dismissal by her mother.

Gina hurried up the stairs. They hadn't argued for some time. Before Deborah left, there had been many late-night discussions; sometimes Gina would crouch at the foot of the steps, listening, waiting to catch them talking about her. But it was usually about Deborah and the myriad of ways her distance caused them worry. They never seemed to think about Gina much at all.

5

The next morning, Gina finished her second cup of coffee and decided. She padded into the kitchen in her slippers. Near the telephone, she kept a copy of the company directory. Two-thirds from the top was Nehra Phillips. She dialed the number.

A man answered, his voice cheerful and high-pitched. "Happy Saturday."

"Hello, is Nehra home?"

"She's run to the store," he said. "This is her husband."

"Oh, sorry." She ran her fingers through her hair, squeezing at the roots. "Hello, Tom. This is Gina, from Mr. Seutter's office?"

"Hello! Nehra's preparing a feast for tonight. We're looking forward to it."

"Thank you for inviting me." She shook her head, cursing inwardly because of course, she had called to cancel.

"Nehra should be back in twenty minutes," Tom said. "Should I have her call?"

"Yes, if you could."

"Will do," he said. "See you this evening."

Gina pushed the red button and dropped the telephone onto the counter.

"It's impossible," she said aloud, and then, "Oh, Ian." She looked at the phone. He hadn't called back last night. What time was it in Korea? Out of the question now, her leaving the condo. She had to be there when he called again.

She crawled back into bed. Her throat was dry, and she had a mild headache. Sunlight filtered through the curtains, gaining strength. Relaxing against the cool sheets, she pulled the blanket over her eyes.

When the telephone made its robotic sound, which always felt like an alarm clock whether she was sleeping or not, Gina uncovered her head and sat up. She glanced at her nightstand, but the cordless handset she kept there was missing.

Ian. How long have I been sleeping? Leaving the blue slippers next to the bed, she rushed to the kitchen. "Hello?"

"Hey there, it's Nehra. Tom said you called and Gina, I have to tell you, I almost didn't call you back."

"Why?"

She cleared her throat. "Because I thought you might be calling to cancel. Then I realized you wouldn't do that, because you know I've been looking forward to it. And because, really, it's only a dinner and everybody needs to eat, right?"

"But Ian called."

Nehra exhaled, very loudly. "I know you're picking them up tomorrow. Don't you think a nice dinner will take your mind off it?"

"He called yesterday, from Korea. He said he needs to talk to me." She leaned against the kitchen counter, its sharp edge creasing her lower back.

A short pause. "You think he'll call back?"

"He said so."

"I'm sure you'll hear from him before I need to pick you up. At five, don't forget. I'm expecting you to come, Gina. Paul called earlier to say he's bringing a bottle of wine. He's very nice."

"Who's Paul?" she asked.

Another sigh. "Tom's friend. Remember?"

"But Nehra, I really don't feel comfortable—"

"Everything will be great. See you at five." A blip, then the long, eerie dial tone.

Gina hung up the phone and took a deep breath. *What can I do?* She found the other receiver in the living room and took it back to the bedroom. Slowly, she put on a pair of pants and zipped a light jacket over her pajama top. She had planned to get the car washed but now she'd have to tidy it up herself. Gathering her supplies—roll of paper towels, plastic bag, spray bottle of 409—and leaving her door open to listen for the phone, she headed outside.

The inside of the car was clean already, but she wiped down the dashboard and the door handles. She noticed a chewing gum wrapper in the back seat and as she leaned over to retrieve it, a voice startled her.

"What on earth are you doing?"

Gina emerged, eyes squinting in the sun. Mrs. Spark stood on the grassy area next to the car in a *Coke is Life* shirt and the same sweatpants she'd worn the night before. "Good morning," she said. "I'm cleaning my car."

"Why don't you take it to the car wash?"

"I'm waiting for a phone call."

The old woman leaned into the car. "From your daughter?"

"My brother."

"But he's in Cambodia!"

"Korea, Mrs. Spark. I missed his call yesterday, but he said he'd call back."

"Today?" she asked, her back straightening in creaks.

"I guess so." Gina sprayed the leather seat with 409 and wiped it with a paper towel. Probably would have been better to have proper leather cleaner, but at least it would be disinfected for the baby.

Mrs. Spark looked down the street. An occasional car sped by, its hum rising then fading. The condos were in a newly developed area, off a four-lane street with a 50-mph speed limit. It was a different feel from where Gina grew up, the narrow road crowded with brownstones. Cars parked bumper to bumper on each side of Euclid Street, in the shadows of reaching branches, and the only vehicles that came through were people leaving or returning home. It wasn't a street that led anywhere else as this one was.

For what must have been the twentieth time, Mrs. Spark asked, "How did that laser work out for your brother?"

Gina closed the car door. "He's very happy with it," she said. "Still has 20-20 vision."

"Everybody's doing it now," she said. "You know, my son might."

Yes, she knew. "Do you think he will?"

"Ha! He's afraid of needles, that one."

"I'm not sure they use a needle. Ian said they numb your eye with drops and give you something to relax."

"With a needle," Mrs. Spark said, crossing her arms.

"Maybe," she relented. "But I think Ian had a pill." The old woman could make an argument out of anything. Sometimes, Gina empathized with her neglectful son, a little.

"What's it called?" Mrs. Spark asked.

"Valium, I think."

She shook her head. "No. It's something with laser."

"Oh, the surgery? It's LASIK."

A flock of black birds passed overhead, their shadows peppering the concrete. The rainstorm downtown had already passed through Berwyn by the time Gina had reached home the night before. The final rain for a week, according to the news. This morning was bright and clear, with a few lingering clouds.

"Ian met his wife at the eye doctor's office," Gina said. "Five years ago, now."

"The Chinese girl?" Mrs. Spark asked. "She's an eye doctor?"

"She's Japanese and she's an assistant."

The old woman turned to leave, apparently uninterested. Suddenly, she turned back. "What will they do with the baby for YKK?"

"Y2K," Gina said under her breath.

A vision of Ian and Carrie, back home in their loft apartment, with its high ceilings and drafty rooms, the exposed beams and brick walls, finding a place for the baby, a place where she could be kept warm, Ian and Carrie holding the baby, changing her diaper together as new parents do, cuddling on their high iron bed. Try as she might, Gina couldn't really picture any of it, accustomed as she was to her image of Ian and Carrie walking the streets of downtown Chicago, ducking into a café for a post-dinner drink, taking the 145 bus to the movie theater in the arts complex, one of those foreign films he was always explaining back when they talked more.

"I don't see how a computer mix-up will change anything," she said.

"It's not only computers!" Drops of saliva exploded from Mrs. Spark's mouth, like sparks. "The water supply could dry up. Computers are running everything now. What about electricity? Did you buy candles like I told you? You'll need candles, matches. I have twenty gallons of water already, lined up in the kitchen. You can't expect me to share it, Gina."

"I wouldn't, Mrs. Spark."

She smiled slightly, her bloodless lips straining. "That sounds mean. I'd share with you, but you should have your own. Single women like us need to prepare."

Miserable to be compared to an old woman who spoke to plastic figurines—because Gina knew Mrs. Spark secretly did. Their porches were separated by a mere fifty feet and sometimes, especially early in the morning, she heard the old woman out there, rearranging and shifting, talking in a quiet voice. A much quieter voice than the normal one she used.

"Well, I'm not that worried about Y2K," Gina said. "I keep frozen dinners in the freezer anyway, and I have that Sparkletts."

"Gina, if all hell breaks loose, that water man will not come to bring you a new bottle."

"I'll buy some water," she promised.

This seemed to satisfy Mrs. Spark, who turned and began her scuttle up the walk. Pausing before the steps leading to her porch, she looked across the grass at Gina. "You baby that car," she called back.

Gina's thoughts turned again to Ian, to his loft apartment and what would be done to keep the infant warm. When the first adoption fell through, she had gone to spend an evening with Carrie. Ian was away on business and had asked Gina to stop by because he was worried.

There was an intercom outside the building, which was square and brick and used to be a packaging company. When Gina buzzed, Carrie came down in a baggy sweatshirt, *Michigan* written in faded letters across the front. The skin around her eyes was puffy, and Gina caught a whiff of something like stale bread and vinegar.

At first, they had chatted about their jobs, their families. Carrie had two brothers, still living close to home in Benton Harbor, Michigan, where she grew up. She talked about her hometown, which was built on an area that was swampland until they built a canal and designated it a harbor. It was a swamp to her, she claimed, and always would be. She grew up looking at Lake Michigan and now lived on the other side, but she still couldn't imagine beyond it.

Gina sipped her wine, which Carrie had served in coffee mugs although Gina knew for a fact one of their wedding gifts was a fancy set of glassware. She listened intently, nodding at the appropriate pauses, and they consumed far too much Chardonnay.

Eventually, there was crying (something she'd never been good with) and apologies, then more crying of the stifled and even more pitiful kind. And all of it made Gina increasingly uncomfortable, until she loosened the top button of her blouse and at one point, went to the white-tiled bathroom and splashed water on her face.

That night, Gina told Carrie something Deborah once said: having children was like giving away your heart in pieces. Gina thought maybe this was what Carrie was feeling, even though the blonde baby was never really hers and despite the fact there was plenty of time for them to build a family. She also told Carrie the story about her mother chasing the neighborhood boy, how Helen came back into the house afterwards and calmly drank a glass of iced tea. She told Carrie she had looked up Japan in her father's atlas. And they talked about Ian. The time he had tried to fast for ten days on lemon juice, water, and maple syrup, and couldn't stop thinking about pancakes. After his LASIK surgery, when he said Carrie was the first beautiful thing he saw. Ian was a tonic, even in his absence. The evening ended in strained laughter but some relief, the first and only time Gina had ever been alone with her sister-in-law.

Try as she might, she couldn't entirely dislike Carrie. She did seem a bit spoiled, but Ian was happy, a fact difficult to ignore. Their apartment, however cold, was clean and well-cared-for. Carrie seemed to share Ian's interests, if not his enthusiasm. And now they'd be parents.

Gina tidied up the car as well as she could. The hubcaps were muddy, and rain had left its salty streaks on the blue paint. But the inside was clear of trash and disinfected, so she gathered her supplies and went back inside.

She decided to take a shower and then, if Ian still hadn't called, she'd phone Nehra again to cancel. Gina lingered under the pulsing, hot water. The master bathroom was fitted with everything in the builder's original package: white tiles with white grout, a white sink, and white cupboards. She had considered remodeling—certainly, she had the money—and Mrs. Spark kept her abreast of which neighbors had updated what. But she liked the sparseness of the room. When the house seemed cluttered and crowded with things taking up space, the bathroom was uncomplicated and welcoming.

Gina hadn't shaved her legs for at least two weeks. She propped her left leg up on the small threshold and bent to complete the task. When she straightened up, her eyes clouded with tiny, clear, fish-shaped figures. She pressed one hand to the cool tile, steadying herself. *My heart.* There were times when she experienced this slight dizziness, times when her legs ached in the morning or she had a sharp pain behind her right eye, and all of this she attributed to her heart, to the slight murmur Dr. Tam had pointed out when she started regular visits again downtown, the diagnosis being a confirmation of everything she had believed all along.

Her vision cleared. She shaved the other leg, then two quick swipes under her arms. "It's impossible," she said aloud, thinking again of the dinner at Nehra's.

She pushed her face into the stream of water, letting it tighten and clean her skin. Eyes closed, she reached down and turned it off. And before she opened her eyes, before she could reacquaint herself to the room, to her life, she heard "...lives in California. Now, I've never met the girl, but I guess she's a teacher."

Gina's eyes widened.

"That's nice." An unfamiliar voice.

"It's been about four years and I've never seen her." Mrs. Spark's voice, unmistakable.

"The daughter?"

"Well, who were we talking about?"

A throat, clearing itself. "Of course. I guess I should—"

"Gina keeps to herself pretty much. Never see anybody coming or going. I'm no social butterfly, but it's strange to me. Nice enough lady, helps me out from time to time."

"You seem like a good neighbor."

Mrs. Spark chuckled, a small sound. "I guess I am."

Gina yanked the towel from the rail outside the shower and quickly wrapped it around her torso. Soundlessly, she opened the bathroom door and tiptoed across the living room, leaving small, damp impressions on the carpet. The curtains were opened and when she saw two figures outside, she crouched and crawled to the window closest to Mrs. Spark's condo.

Carefully, she peeked out. A woman with red hair, short in stature, stood next to the gray stone rabbit, while Mrs. Spark leaned on the rail near the metallic bat. The woman kept glancing over her shoulder towards Gina's condo. Gina's wet hair dripped down her neck, making a small puddle between her knees. And then she saw it: the manila envelope tucked under the woman's arm. Was it that nurse, again, after so many phone calls?

Gina dropped to her knees and crawled towards the bathroom, unwilling to risk being seen. After a few awkward movements with the towel, which was cumbersome and kept getting tangled, she took it off and threw it across the room.

The carpet was rough against her knees. She could hear their voices, even with the window closed. "A garage sale last year," and "wouldn't think you could find such a big one," and Gina knew Mrs. Spark was giving the visitor a tour of her porch decorations, where they were purchased and so on. She knew the tour well.

The slack skin of her belly pulled and stretched, and her rear end flexed as she crawled. She felt the cool air now. Her breasts, heavy and awkward. At the door to the bathroom, a thought occurred to her, so she crossed the living room again, hands and knees, all the way to the front door, where she carefully kneeled upright and turned the bolt. Slowly, quietly. Mrs. Spark had ears like a bat when she wanted to listen.

Back in the bathroom, Gina dried off and applied her lotion in the usual way, although she was rushed and kept looking at the high, open window. She put her clothes on. The women continued to speak, mostly Mrs. Spark.

She stepped back into the shower and slid the window so that it was open only an inch.

The voices were moving.

"Maybe she's leaving," Gina whispered.

And then, three loud knocks on the door. Her door. Like a trapped animal, her eyes darted from side to side. She stepped out of the shower, sat on the closed toilet and waited.

Three more knocks, muffled voices.

Four knocks in a different rhythm. Knock. Knock. Knock. Knock.

"Gina?" Mrs. Spark called with her raspy voice.

She crossed her arms, shivering a bit.

The voices grew smaller, then louder again as they approached Mrs. Spark's porch and Gina's bathroom window.

"I can't imagine where she could be," Mrs. Spark said. "Her car is here."

"Don't worry," the woman said. "I'll leave this in her mailbox. That's what I said I'd do."

"She was here this morning," the old woman continued. "She's in there, I know it."

"Mrs. Spark, I think—"

"You know, I could take it for you."

Gina's breath caught. Surely, after the efforts this woman had made, after the many times she'd called, the messages and the visit yesterday, surely, she wouldn't—

"That's a good idea," the woman said. "I'd feel better knowing someone will personally deliver it."

"Oh, you can count on me," Mrs. Spark said.

Gina hurried down the hall, dropped to her knees and crawled quickly to the front window, in time to see Mrs. Spark waving a gnarled hand, clutching in the other the manila envelope. She crawled to the door and peered through the window there. A silver car backed out of the parking space next to hers, turned and waited a moment at the exit, its right turn signal blinking a farewell before it entered the street.

Her hand shook as she dropped the curtain. She knelt by the door. A few moments later, another knock sounded, so loud and close to her ear that she almost cried out.

"Gina." Mrs. Spark's voice came through the closed door. Gina could picture her colorless lips, her pale face leaning forward. "She's gone," the old woman said.

At the place where the kitchen tile met carpet, there was a small tear, a few fibers poking up from the dividing metal strip. Gina stared at this flaw in the carpet. She'd never noticed it before.

Three angry knocks.

Muttering, a shuffling of feet down the steps. The snap of Mrs. Spark's door. Gina crawled to the kitchen.

The mini bottle of Myer's Rum was dark brown, with a label awash in warm colors. A golden background accented with leafy plants, a foreground of reddish barrels. In the back, near water (although it was hard to tell if it was water), there was a long, squat building with a red roof. And it was this roof, this cottage, that always reminded Gina of a rare family trip, the summer she was eight, before her mother became pregnant with Ian. They may have taken more trips if her brother hadn't been born, but she'd never held it against him.

They had loaded up their car, a four-door, white Ford. Gina couldn't remember the name of the model now, had never thought about the car much until she bought her own. One of the many things she wished she could ask her mother. At the time, the Ford was only a couple of years old, with beige leather seats, whitewall tires, and little, metal ashtrays where they'd stuff their trash. They drove two hours to a campground in Wisconsin where they'd rented a cabin next to Aunt Klara and Uncle Pete. Their cousin, Roxana, was three years older than Deborah but would play with them when no one else was around.

Bits and pieces from the trip: tramping through the woods with Deborah and Roxana, the cold, rushing water of the river, the evening dinners, usually in the clearing between the two cabins. Aunt Klara had made friends with a younger couple and many nights, they'd have dinner together. Gina remembered the lively discussions amongst the adults, and the developing body Roxana showed them, in glimpses, behind the cabin. Smiling faces around a campfire and one night, a flame singed her father's pant leg, the type of accident that at home would have ended in harsh words and a retreat to his reading chair. On vacation, the incident evoked fits of laughter and teasing from her mother, who was radiant in her checkered top and calf-length pants. All of them happy and youthful in the firelight.

Within two years, Ian was born, and Aunt Klara moved with her family to Atlanta. Summers were spent around the house and neighborhood. Deborah knew several girls on Euclid Street and when she was in a generous mood, she invited Gina along. There was Grandma Sahlin's house for afternoon grapefruit juice and Proksa Park with its shelter of trees. But they never took another family vacation, not once.

The times her father acted out of character jumped out, demanding attention in ways other memories did not. The trip to Wisconsin, when her parents seemed almost to be courting, the times he emerged from the family room to raise his voice, the evening he talked on and on about Elvis Presley, even humming a few bars of *Blue Christmas* to the table of grinning faces.

Gina finished the Myer's Rum, having poured it into a mug of hot cocoa to ration her club soda. Her hair was still damp at the roots, but she didn't want Mrs. Spark to hear the blow dryer. She opened the refrigerator, looked into the cupboards, and took inventory. At least six or seven days, she figured, maybe more. She could keep herself locked in for some time.

6

Carefully, Gina closed the kitchen blinds and put her glass into the dishwasher. She felt calmer and more in control. She walked back to the bathroom, where the telephone sat by the sink. She pressed the green button to hear the steady hum of the dial tone, then pressed the red button.

It occurred to her, in an emergency Ian may have called their sister. True, the two of them weren't close. Deborah often complained because Ian had never been to Sacramento, even when he was still single and had plenty of vacation time from the paper company. Ian said she was busy carting the boys around and didn't have time for him anyway.

Gina clearly saw the chasm between her siblings but had no idea how to bridge it. She could deal with each separately, with Deborah's self-interests and Ian's myriad of interests, with Deborah's insistences and Ian's boundlessness. She was closer to Ian because it felt like they had grown up together, even though she and Deborah were only a year apart, and an entire decade separated her from her baby brother.

For the first time in months, Gina wanted to talk to her sister. She took the telephone to her bedroom and opened the closet door. When she saw the rows of shoes—black, brown, blue, mostly low-heeled—she had the bracing thought they were all the same. Different colors, but the same conservative cut, the same dull leather. She moved aside several pairs and ducked into the closet. With her free hand, she pulled the door closed, leaving only a crack of fresh air and light. She dialed Deborah's number and balanced the phone on her shoulder.

Deborah answered on the third ring. "Hello?"

"It's Gina."

"What?"

"It's me," she said, a little more loudly.

"Any word from Ian?" Deborah's voice was calm and measured, an opposite to Gina's ragged breath and racing heart.

"Only a voice message. You haven't heard from him?"

"Me? No. I wonder if they have the baby yet."

Gina leaned against the closet wall. "They saw her yesterday, he said on the message."

"Yes, but to *have* her," Deborah said. "You can't imagine what it's like to hold your first child." She sighed again. "I bet she's adorable."

In Gina's experience, babies didn't look like much until later, when their features began to take hold.

"Just a minute." Deborah covered the receiver and Gina heard muffled voices. "That was Justin. He's going to drive Jared to his football practice for me. He got a new car, well, *we* got him a car. You can't afford a car payment working at Subway."

"He sounds grown up," Gina said.

"His voice changed," she whispered. "You haven't seen them for a few years."

Outside, a car sped by and even from the closet, Gina could hear the ticking of the living room clock. "You should come for a visit," she said.

"Why?"

"I feel like you never came home because of Daddy. Your big fight. But that was a long time ago."

"What do you mean? I came home for Christmas every year on my school breaks. I spent that one summer before I met Dan. I've been to the city several times."

"I've been thinking about when he died, how sudden it was."

"Do you know why we fought?" Deborah asked.

"I always thought it was because he didn't want you to leave."

"Are you kidding? They were on my case about college all the time, Dad especially. To tell you the truth, schoolwork came easily for me most of the time."

"Must be nice," Gina muttered. At the junior college, the only class where she didn't feel completely lost was an office skills elective. There, she learned to type, file, and organize. After one semester, she transferred to a secretarial school and finished in fourteen months.

"The fight," Deborah said, "was about you."

"What do you mean?"

"I told Dad they should encourage you more. About college, about everything."

Gina shook her head. "That wasn't your business."

"That's what he said. I think what they really thought was that I should have—I don't know—guided you more."

"Oh."

"But Gina, don't you remember Dad's funeral? I was there. It was terrible for me. You know that."

"It was terrible for everyone."

"For a long time, I felt guilty for leaving," Deborah said. "How was I supposed to know what would happen?"

"At least you were close to him," Gina said. "Before that, I mean."

Deborah cleared her throat. "I don't know what gave you the impression we were close. Was he close to anyone, except maybe Mom at one time? He loved his books and magazines. I mean, I know he loved us. Everyone loves their family. But I'm not sure I knew much about him, which sounds funny when you're talking about your father, when you're talking about someone you lived with for twenty years." She paused. "Did you know him?"

Gina's face flushed. "Of course. He was kind and sometimes funny."

"Funny? When?"

"I can't think of an exact time." She stretched her leg and inadvertently, kicked the closet door. "I was invited to a dinner tonight."

"That's nice."

"My friend is introducing me to a man."

"A man?"

"But I'm worried about missing Ian's call."

Deborah laughed. "Gina, I know you. You were waiting for an excuse not to go."

"It's important, Ian's trip."

"I know. Listen, I have an appointment in twenty minutes and haven't done a thing with myself."

"I'll let you—"

"Please tell Ian to call me, or call me yourself, when they're back with the baby."

"I will."

"And Gina?"

"What?"

"Go to the dinner. Ian's a big boy now."

The dial tone buzzed, insistent and reliable. Gina peeked around the closet door. The alarm clock on her nightstand beeped two red dots between the jointed numbers. Almost lunchtime.

In her quietest moments and sometimes in her dreams, Gina went over the details of the places where she had lived. Not the events that had taken place or the things said while living there, but the actual architecture of the building, the layout of the rooms and furnishings. She'd close her eyes, draw a mental picture of her condominium, and it would calm her. She knew, like she knew her own hands and face, that the living room was two-thirds of a long rectangle, with the kitchen making up the remaining third. The rest, another long rectangle comprised of the dining area, the hallway and bath, and her bedroom—in total, a near perfect square.

Gina's first apartment was a recurring setting for her dreams; she lived there for three years before moving back home after her father died. She spent nine years in the brownstone near her mother's, after she moved out again, but she had almost no memories of the character of that place. She did remember a long, L-shaped crack in the cement on the front porch, which made her think of people who read hands to tell the future. This is your lifeline, they always said in the movies. In the kitchen of the brownstone, there was a corner near the stove where the wallpaper was peeling. A print of peonies that should have been in a bedroom, a child's room. Gina sat in the mornings with her cup of coffee and imagined scooting a chair over to the corner and giving the wallpaper a tug. But she never did.

She could recall Grandma Sahlin's fragrant home, each sitting surface velvety and cool, lace doilies on every table and the blonde wood of her kitchen cupboards, which was unlike the dark lacquered surfaces of most homes back then.

There was her childhood home, her apartment, the brownstone, and almost four years ago, she had purchased her condo. But the first apartment was the place most visited in her mind: the shaded patio, the closet with its gleaming, sliding doors. The bathroom had a gold faucet with inlaid white enamel handles and clawed feet supporting the bathtub. When the window was open, she could hear the poplar and ash trees whooshing and snapping in the wind.

Her employer's home was another place she could call to mind from memory, although she usually thought of the panoramic view rather than the place itself. Along the entire length of the living space were floor to ceiling windows affording a vivid vista of the street and beyond that, Lake Michigan. During the summer while they vacationed, she went over on her lunch hour to check on the place and bring in the mail. Strange that she had been to Mr.

Seutter's home so many times, and he would never see hers. She flushed to think of him standing on the porch of her condo now, as she burrowed in her closet hidden by shirts and pleated pants, surrounded by piles of similar shoes.

Gina's bones creaked as she rose and opened the closet door. She found Nehra's number on the work directory and called. Six rings and an answering machine picked up.

Hello, you have reached the Phillips'. Leave your name and number, or we won't be able to call you back! Bye now!

She waited five minutes and tried again. Answering machine. She hung up. She waited ten more minutes and called. Answering machine. This time, she left a message asking Nehra to call back. On an impulse, she called back five minutes after that. Answering machine.

It was such a bother, having friends. Aside from the occasional chat at work, Gina couldn't really see the point of it. She didn't mind being alone, not really. She found plenty to do.

Nehra was the only one at work who Gina considered a good friend. She'd bring almond cookies from her special grocery store and throughout the day, she'd stop by to chat, always in consideration that Gina's priority was Mr. Seutter. Nehra was the only one who came to her mother's funeral, three years ago now in 1996, a beautiful sunny day in June, the month of weddings.

Gina tapped the phone against her leg. She'd try again in five minutes.

In the days leading up to Helen's death, Ian had unraveled a bit. For the first time in his life, he lost weight. His sweaters puckered and hung; dark circles shadowed his eyes. He told his sisters many things about funeral practices and dying. He said Hindus believe dying is like falling asleep and in this way, everyone has experienced death many times. The astral body separates from the physical body, exactly like during sleep, only in death the silver cord connecting the two breaks. Ian wanted to move Helen's bed, so her head faced the east. He wanted her to resolve unfinished business to avoid bad karma. Deborah said their mother's karma was her own business and pressed her lips together exactly the way Helen would have done. Gina, on the other hand, always remembered the bit about the silver cord and found it helpful sometimes to picture her mother floating towards the clouds, gripping a shiny piece of rope, becoming smaller and smaller and most importantly, freed from her failing body. She had to think this process was a private one, that her mother would not be forced to float amidst other astral bodies, because a group expedition like that would look alarmingly like Standing Out, something Helen couldn't abide.

The memorial service was non-denominational; they'd never been regular churchgoers. Grandma Sahlin quite possibly turned in her own grave that day, witnessing her daughter, baptized Catholic, sent off without a priest present. Ian and Carrie wore white. Carrie had her long black hair pinned back on one side with a spray of white flowers. When Gina asked Ian about their clothing, he said it was a custom but didn't elaborate whose. Propped on the coffin was a portrait of their mother taken in the late seventies, all glossy hair and skin airbrushed to perfection. It looked like her and it didn't. After a few words were spoken by the eulogist, they gathered in the lobby, where Ian whispered to a Tibetan monk who had come for a plate of fruit and a check. Her brother had tried to cover every possible base, as far as their mother's eternity was concerned. Deborah stewed in the corner, her irritation with Ian providing a convenient distraction from grief.

Gina watched both of her siblings, took the whole scene in. And the worst of it, the absolute distressing truth of that day, as much as she wanted to push the evidence out of her mind, through the greeting and smiling and thanking, she wanted it to be over. And worse yet, she had felt that way even before her mother died.

It was so different from her father's lightning-strike exit, when no one was ready, and the entire week passed in a fog of disbelief. No, they lost their mother in a prolonged series of smaller losses, one after the other.

Four-fifteen.

Gina, hands trembling again, picked up the phone and called Nehra's number, which she now had memorized. Answering machine.

Hello, you have reached the Phillips'. Leave your name and number, or we won't be able to call you back! Bye now!

The sun was fading outside, not yet retreating but losing its vigor.

A click, monotonous droning, seven beeps.

Hello, you have reached the Phillips'. Leave your name and number, or we won't be able to call you back! Bye now!

Between calls, Gina pulled a brush through her hair and put on two swipes of lipstick. She changed shirts and stepped into a pair of medium-heeled shoes. In the kitchen, she poured vodka into the last of the club soda, hardly fizzy anymore, and sat at the dining room table.

Hello, you have reached the Phillips'. Leave your name and number, or we won't be able to call you back! Bye now!

As the clock ticked menacingly from its vantage point, Gina sipped and waited, sipped and waited, not sure what to expect first.

7

Berwyn, January 1977

Downstairs, the front door thumped shut; her mother had left. Gina splashed water on her face. She looked the same as she had the day before. Thin, pinkish lips with the hint of two front teeth even when her mouth was closed. Rounded shoulders and smooth hands. Here, a streak of reddish freckles across the line of her cheekbone. The same brown eyes, her hair cut into a simple bob she kept tucked behind each ear. In her abdomen, a steady pulsing.

Ian had left with their mother to attend a birthday party. There had been much discussion about the party for several days, Ian wondering how he'd handle the roller-skating, Helen contemplating a gift that would please but not overwhelm the first truly close friend her boy had made. This lack of a best friend seemed to bother Helen more than it ever did Ian. Several boys in the neighborhood stopped by occasionally and Ian never complained of loneliness or Not Fitting In. Helen's impressions of what childhood should be were colored by Deborah's joyride through hers. Always surrounded by admirers, always at the center of something, girls in and out of the house like it was a department store sale.

The Midwest had been hit with a large storm early in the new year, and the snow stayed for over a week. Small storms followed the first, keeping the yards and roofs white and sparkling under the streetlights. One afternoon, Ian found Gina, worrying and staring on her bed, and talked her into going outside to see something he'd been doing with a couple of the neighbor boys. Two brothers, both younger than Ian, but what did that matter? At twelve years old, Ian could make himself comfortable with anyone.

Gina put on her coat, gloves, and boots and followed him to Proksa Park, where in one corner under a canopy of trees, they'd built an igloo. It was like something from a dream, this icy structure in the middle of the familiar park, where she and Ian had picnicked when he was younger, where she once fell from her bike and was helped to her feet by two old women who then scolded her.

Gina walked around the igloo, amazed. The boys ducked through the oval-shaped opening, rimmed with snow, like salt on a margarita glass. She touched the cold, slippery surface. The igloo was about five feet tall and eight feet wide, the snow packed and smoothed to ice, the floor of the thing tramped down with handfuls of branches. Ian pulled her inside, where the three boys crouched, their breath like the excited pants of dogs, crystalline in the frosty air, everything around them pure white and clean.

Ian's face, flushed and grinning. His brown eyes so alive. "I can't leave this place," he said.

In the bathroom mirror, Gina looked at her own eyes now, a middling version of Ian's vivid ones. Nobody had to worry about Ian or his chances. Anyone who could make something like that igloo—

Footsteps below. Her father's shoes on the wooden floor, into the kitchen then back out. She imagined him settling back onto his chair and when she finally gathered herself and went downstairs, that's exactly where she found him.

"Daddy?"

He looked up from the newspaper, which was spread and bent to form a tent around him.

Gina stood beside his chair. "I wanted to ask you something."

He removed his glasses but held them in his fist. "What is it?"

"I think I need to see a doctor."

"But your mother's not here."

"I didn't want to tell her."

Something flashed across his face, a vague understanding, and for some reason, it made him handsome. At forty-six years old, his skin was unlined and with his glasses off, he looked even younger. His dark hair was still thick and straight, his shoulders beginning to droop. Henry's complexion was darker than anyone else's, a fact Helen often brought up when talking about his Yugoslavian ancestors. But his cultural connections were further buried than hers were. Helen's own mother was born in Sweden, whereas his closest non-American relative was a few generations back. They made a striking couple, Gina's mother with her fair skin and blonde hair, her father with his more serious, darker look.

"I'll call Dr. Trainor." He began to lift the newspaper from his lap.

"Can we go today?" Gina asked.

He looked at her fully then. Thirty minutes later, they were sputtering down the driveway in his car. The front seat was cluttered with papers and used coffee cups. He was the only one who ever rode in it.

Dr. Trainor's office was several blocks away, in a former residential zone that had been changed into small businesses, mostly doctors' offices. Gina remembered coming as a child for check-ups and minor illnesses, but it had been several years since she'd seen the doctor. Dr. Trainor and her father had attended college together, where they wound up in the same history class, although both were bound for quite different disciplines. Gina's father completed a business degree and went to work for insurance companies and eventually, for himself as a public adjuster. Much like an attorney, he assessed losses and advocated for the policy holder. David against Goliath, he often joked, and many days when he shuffled up the front steps after work, he certainly had the embattled air of the underdog. Dr. Trainor had two daughters close in age to Gina and Deborah, although the families rarely met over the years.

In the small lobby, her father spoke to Roberta, Dr. Trainor's long-time receptionist. She was heavyset, with auburn hair pulled back into a loose bun. Gina sat on one of the scratchy upholstered chairs in the waiting room, trying not to notice the concerned glances Roberta snuck her way. The office smelled as it always had, like the cologne section of Walgreens, coated with the gritty residue of cigarette smoke. She remembered that in each of the examination rooms, a different painting of a beach was hung. One room had Atlantic City, one Daytona, and she couldn't remember the third.

Her father removed his coat and folded it over his elbow. Sitting in the chair next to hers, he reached over to the stack of magazines on the nearby table. Thumbing quickly through, he chose a *Newsweek*, a special Inauguration edition which promised information on the new government, the festivities, the power brokers, and even a talk with Rosalynn. Gina knew that her father liked President Carter and her mother didn't, and from what Gina had seen of him on the television—his thoughtfulness, his soft-spoken speaking style—it made some sort of sense.

"Gina?"

She looked up and Patricia, another long-time employee of Dr. Trainor's, stood in the open doorway. Behind her, the carpeted hallway stretched, plain and empty, with two doors visible on either side. The three exam rooms and Dr. Trainor's office.

Gina followed her into the last room on the right. A metal sink, the large leather examining table covered in paper and at the head, in plastic, and the trash basket stuffed with paper gowns and tissues.

"How have you been, dear?" Patricia squinted through the blue and purple speckled frames of her glasses. Another middle-aged woman, with soft edges and a dimple at each elbow. Gina wondered if young people looked all the same to them. She motioned to the scale in the corner and Gina stepped onto it.

"One hundred and forty-nine," she said, making a note on her folder. She patted the papered end of the chair and Gina climbed up. Blood pressure next, the assured press of the cuff until it almost hurt, then the whoosh as it let go.

"A little low," Patricia said.

Gina crossed her arms over her chest and looked up at the painting on the wall, which was really a print of a painting under glass, the colors more muted than she remembered. Pismo Beach.

Patricia left her alone. Gina scooted back and laid her head on the cushioned plastic. She turned onto her side and brought her knees up. She was so tired, had hardly slept for days.

She hadn't told the broker anything; in fact, they hadn't spoken for weeks. The averted gazes in the break room, the quick detours when they saw each other in the hall or lobby, all that was left. After their final date, she had called him a few times, trying to understand what had caused the rift. And he acted like she was harassing him and started avoiding her in earnest. It was humiliating, infuriating.

The door opened and Dr. Trainor came in. Tall, all angles and folds of white, with a salt-and-pepper moustache she didn't remember. His hands protruded like the roots of a tree; the backs covered with coarse hair.

"Look at you, Gina," he said. "A grown woman now."

As she sat up, the paper crinkled underneath her.

"Twenty-three?" he asked, looking at the folder.

"Yes,' she said.

He lowered himself onto the round stool at her feet. His long legs folded outward like a frog. "Your father tells me you've followed him into insurance."

"I'm a secretary," she said.

"And Deborah, how is she?"

"She's graduating college," Gina said. "Has a boyfriend."

He ran his fingers over his moustache. "Wonderful," he said. "I still see Ian for his regular check-ups, so I won't ask about him."

"He's great," Gina said.

"Yes." He scooted back on the wheeled scooter. "Gina, what brings you in today?"

Her face flooded with heat. She looked over his head at Pismo Beach, at the smooth line where the water met sand. "I've missed my period."

"Ah," he said.

"It was due three weeks ago. One time, I thought I felt it, but no."

"Sometimes because of stress," he said, "a young woman will get off schedule."

She looked at him, at his eyebrows raised over the black glasses and there was something so familiar about that look, something like her father's way of peering over a book or newspaper. She didn't say anything.

"Have you felt anything different?" he asked.

Instead of her body, of which Gina was still in large ways mostly unaware, she thought about the feeling of dread she experienced each morning. She had once been so comfortable at her job, so proud of her skills and the appreciation she received, but now she spent her days crouched behind her typewriter, wondering if the other secretaries were talking about her whenever they gathered at the coffee pot or outside to smoke. She worried about the broker and what he might have told them; she worried about his wife and whether she'd visit the office.

"Soreness in your breasts? Dizziness? Nausea?"

She shook her head.

Dr. Trainor stood up and motioned for her to lie back. His large hands pressed into her abdomen, exploring the deep area beside each hipbone. She held her breath. He pressed the stethoscope against her chest, moving it here and there, placing his free hand over his ear, leaning closer.

"Have I ever mentioned your heart, Gina?" he asked.

She couldn't immediately process what he had said, being so preoccupied with the other thing. "What?"

"You've got a slight murmur," he said. "Do you know what that is?"

"No," she said.

He towered over the examining table, the large, leathered monstrosity that reminded Gina of her father's recliner.

"Here's the thing, dear." He put a hand on her knee, and she was strangely comforted by the contact. "If you think pregnancy is a possibility, we can do a urine test. But you'd have to wait until later today for the results. The lab is across town, and we take the samples over after lunch." He took his hand off and grabbed the folder again. He asked her the date of her last period and she told him. He flipped through a few pages and looked at her again. "I can do a quick exam," he said, "if you think it's a possibility."

She crossed her arms over her chest, fighting the urge to cross her legs. "Okay."

Paper ruffling and sticking, heels in cold metal, the stretching, the cold air, the cold metal inside and finally, a pinching that made her catch her breath.

"All done," he said.

Her knees clunked together and awkwardly holding the paper gown, she moved back to a sitting position.

Dr. Trainor stood at the metal sink washing his hands, first with soap, then a rinse under the steady stream of water, then soap again. She got the impression he was stalling having to face her.

But when he turned, his face was kind and relaxed. "A heart murmur," he said, "is an arrhythmia of the heart. Too much blood flows through the heart at once, or it flows more quickly than normal. Sometimes it can indicate other problems."

A soft knock sounded on the door and after Dr. Trainor responded, Patricia stuck her head in. She avoided looking at Gina. "Sorry for the interruption, Doctor. Lettie's on the phone."

One of his daughters, Gina remembered. The younger one.

Dr. Trainor looked at her. "Lettie's at college in Virginia. Sorry, Gina. I'll have to take it."

She sat in a flurry of emotion, her thoughts bounding from her heart to her lower body and back again, an entire torso of uncertainty. And below, a small ache from the exam.

After several minutes, Dr. Trainor came back in. His face was shiny, his hair mussed. "Gina, so sorry." He leaned against the sink and shook his head. "Lettie's been causing us some worry, that's all, so I can relate to your—" He paused.

"What about my heart?" she asked.

He seemed to have gathered himself and approached her. His hand went again to her knee, but his eyes had a faraway look. "You have to be careful, that's all. You'll be okay this time, Gina. But you should take care this doesn't happen again. Do you understand?"

She nodded, although she didn't understand at all. This time, his hand felt controlling, and she wanted him to step away and give her space.

He did. He took the folder with its hieroglyphic marks and left.

And none of it made sense to her until later that evening, when the steady, pulsing pain turned into something more definitive, when she stood in a steamy shower with a rusty taste in her mouth and hands turned upwards to catch the warm stream as the first bits of blood spattered between her feet. Dark, kidney-bean fragments, a rope of reddish gel, more blood, and she felt her heart thrashing, could almost hear it except for the static spray of water, the droplets hitting her chest like small explosions. She pressed her face against the cool tile until the rest had washed away and the realization came to her: the baby was gone, her baby, Dr. Trainor had made sure of it, and because of her injured heart and its inability to regulate itself, there would never be another. She understood everything.

8

Later, when the whole thing was over, Gina would think back to that Saturday and stop the action, break down the day into a series of occurrences: cleaning her car, the overheard discussion between Sandra Pierce, R.N., and Mrs. Spark, fortification in her condo, the conversations with Deborah, many futile phone calls to Nehra, the final knock at her door and everything that came spilling afterwards. If she suspended the flow between these scenes, if she had done something a little bit differently, would everything have turned out the same? She could have faced the nurse. She might have avoided Nehra's dinner. Every single part of your life could be analyzed and reanalyzed, back to the very beginning, your parents' gametes forming the zygote that became you.

As it was, she was tired of hiding. No point in avoiding anything. If she had to be honest, maybe in some small way she was curious about what the night had in store for her. Mostly, she gave up fighting. That's how Gina found herself standing at her front door, staring at four people. In front was Nehra, smiling with flashes of worry in her eyes, and her husband, Tom. Slightly taller than Nehra, his reddish complexion was topped with thinning blonde hair, and he seemed to have grown stouter since Gina had last seen him. In the back, a man with dark glasses loomed on the lower porch step. He seemed very tall, at least six feet, and rail thin. And beside him, with a faded, red kerchief framing glittering eyes, Mrs. Spark leaned forward in a familiar, searching way. Under her arm was the manila envelope.

Nehra spoke first. "Sorry to invade like this, Gina. We've been at the farmer's market, and picked up Paul on the way back." She wore a purple dress with sequins around the collar and a patent leather belt, which she kept adjusting. Gina felt underdressed in her slacks and blouse, even though she had worn the higher heels. "Can we use your restroom?" Nehra asked. "The ones at the market, well—"

"Please, come in." She held the door while they walked by, one after the other.

"Nice place," Tom said when they all stood in the living room.

"My unit is exactly the same," Mrs. Spark announced.

Nehra gripped Gina's arm and turned her towards the tall man. "This is Paul. Paul, Gina."

Gina shook his hand firmly, as she had seen Amanda Blevin do when she was running a meeting. "Nice to meet you, Paul."

His hand was cool and bony.

"If you're sure you don't mind," Nehra asked.

"Not at all. Around the corner there, on the right."

Mrs. Spark took a short walk around the living room, looking into corners. She turned around and held out the envelope. "Gina, the nurse left this for you." Her eyebrows were raised, two tufts of gray.

"Thank you," Gina put it on the cabinet.

"Don't you want to take a look?" Mrs. Spark looked at Tom and Paul. "This nurse has been searching for Gina, leaving her messages."

"It's only old medical records, Mrs. Spark." She shrugged, gave the men a dismissive frown.

"Why didn't you want them?" the old woman persisted.

Nehra emerged from the hallway. "Your turn, Tom." She motioned with her thumb, and he rounded the corner towards the bathroom. She looked at Gina's shoes. "You look nice," she said. "Ready to go?"

"Ian hasn't called back," Gina told her.

Nehra turned to Paul. "Her brother is in Korea, adopting a baby. I'm sure if it was important enough, he would've called."

"I don't know," she said. "I feel like I should wait."

Paul walked over to a houseplant on the kitchen counter. He pulled out the arrow-shaped plastic piece with instructions for the plant's care and began to read it.

"I suppose I'll let you young people get to your dinner," Mrs. Spark said. "My son might come tomorrow. His wife's gone out of town with her friends." She rolled her eyes for Gina's benefit.

"Wait," Nehra said as the old woman reached the door. "I have an idea. You have a cordless phone, right, Gina?"

She nodded.

"I'm sure the reception would reach to Mrs. Spark's house." Nehra looked back and forth between them. "I'll give Mrs. Spark my phone number and you give her your phone. If your brother calls while you're gone, she can have him call my house."

Gina shook her head. "Oh, no, I couldn't ask her to do that." Mrs. Spark had been in her business enough recently.

"It's perfect," Nehra insisted.

"I don't mind," Mrs. Spark said.

"Where did you get this?" Paul said.

The three women looked over.

"The plant?" Gina asked.

"Yes."

"The supermarket," she said.

"Strange," he said. "This is a Firecracker Flower. See here, the orange blooms? You usually don't see these in such a cold climate."

Gina looked toward Nehra, who was conspicuously avoiding her glance.

Paul pulled a leather wallet from his back pocket and opened it. "I have a card here, the blooming schedules of different types of flowers. It's listed by type and then name."

As he flipped through a tri-fold laminated card, Gina threw a more purposeful glare in Nehra's direction.

"That's interesting," Mrs. Spark piped up.

Tom returned from the restroom. "Ready, everyone? It's gonna take an hour at least for the brisket."

"Where's your phone, Gina?" Mrs. Spark asked, her eyes wide.

Gina handed it over. She got her purse and followed everyone outside. The sun was descending, liquid orange over the horizon.

They watched as Mrs. Spark bounded up her steps and entered her condo. She had Gina's white telephone tucked under her arm in place of the envelope.

"You boys get in the car," Nehra said. "I want to speak to Gina for a minute."

"Don't take too long, Mommy," Tom said.

"I won't."

Gina had forgotten about Tom's nickname for Nehra.

Nehra grabbed her by both arms. "I'm sorry, but I couldn't wait until we got to the house."

"What?"

"We've been friends six years, right?"

Gina looked up to the sky, did the math. "Yes."

Nehra's eyes narrowed. "Then explain to me how it's possible you have a daughter I don't know about?"

Air escaped Gina as though she had been kicked. She could strangle her nosy neighbor. "I don't have a daughter."

Nehra let go of Gina's arms and crossed her own. Her hair wasn't as spiky today and the copper color was softer in the twilight. "Mrs. Spark said your daughter lives in California. She told all of us."

"In case you hadn't noticed, she's not the most stable old woman."

She frowned. "I don't understand."

"Wait," Gina said. "Why were you talking to her?"

"You've talked about her," Nehra said. "We're trying to plan a big party for your twentieth anniversary at work. I wanted to see if she could help me with addresses, you know, your family and friends. You keep that goddamn Rolodex locked up at work!"

"Those are Mr. Seutter's contacts!" Gina motioned to the car. "They're staring!"

Nehra's eyes didn't leave her face. "But I don't—"

Tom started the car and the engine thrummed healthily.

"Let's go," Gina said.

Nehra opened her mouth then closed it. They walked together towards the car and as they reached it, she pinched the soft flesh under Gina's upper arm. "This isn't over."

In the backseat of the car, Paul's knees splayed awkwardly to each side. His hair was thick and black, shiny with some type of styling cream and combed straight back from his broad forehead. Gazing at them through his square glasses, he tapped his fingers on the armrest.

Nehra twisted around in her seat. "Gina, you should have seen the farmer's market! We got some beautiful avocadoes. Tom's going to make guacamole for us." She looked at her, then Paul. "We got asparagus, apples, some large-leaf spinach. Gina, does your brother still make those veggie drinks?"

A while back, Ian had purchased an expensive blender. He had made the purchase without Carrie's consent and for some time, he used it to make the juice blends that were supposed to replace two of his three daily meals.

"I don't think he's doing that anymore," Gina told her.

. Gina talked about work and her small role. Tom presented the brisket, in slices surrounded by its own juices.

a had two helpings of the meat and was having a good time. A third wine was opened, another red, and the foursome quit the table. She ghtly as she rose, her head spinning as she helped Nehra move dishes table to the kitchen. Bright lights overhead. Nehra giggling and the scalloped potatoes had been left in the oven. Smoke and black aking pan. Everyone laughing, the sound in a container now. Gina st the counter, hot in her blouse, the one with the ivory buttons that of her mother and Not Standing Out, and the men in and out of randishing the tools from the grill to soak in the sink and carrying ke scepters, and Nehra coaxing everyone out of the kitchen and room, where Tom immediately went to a brown leather recliner her wine glass near its twin, leaving a plaid loveseat for Gina and

e to her. The square glasses, the tall frame, the hair combed for minded her of Dr. Trainor, former employer of Sandra Pierce, nd her family doctor until that one time. Only in appearance however. Tall, thin, ropey arms and square shoulders. But easy, Dr. Trainor had been authoritative.

ting into the expensive blouse, panicked as she suddenly ess phone, losing its charge in Mrs. Spark's house (if it hadn't Gina rose to return to the kitchen, where Nehra still made e promising she'd straighten up in the morning. Tom looked mething she might need, but there was nothing to be done something about her heart and looked back, then tripped, ry-style coffee table, the legs of which folded under the ntering rupture, and she landed on her side amidst the

"It sure was a good idea," Nehra said. "Today there was a man giving a demonstration on veggie drinks. You can get your daily allowance of vitamins in one tasty glass."

"Explain to me how spinach and carrots blended into a liquid would be tasty," Tom said.

"You use fruit too," she said. "To give it a little sugar."

"Mommy," he said. "You'd buy anything and everything if I wasn't around to watch out for you."

She punched Tom playfully in the arm, while Gina and Paul shifted in the back.

They chatted all the way, mostly Nehra but with occasional contributions from the rest. Soon, they pulled into a long driveway that curved towards a white, aluminum-sided house. Two trees stood like sentries on either side of the driveway, framing the garage door, which Tom opened with the button of his remote. Once parked, Gina squeezed out and stepped around cases of canned food stacked in the corner of the garage. Paul was waiting to let her pass on the other side of the car, a questionable gallantry since she had to squeeze between him and the car, and she inadvertently brushed against him with the front of her blouse.

By the time they got settled inside, Tom had already been in the backyard. He returned to the kitchen now, a waft of smoke and lighter fluid trailing him.

All at once, a flurry of gray and white fur, a cacophony of clicking on the tile floor. Nehra's two dogs jumped and wriggled, and they all watched as she greeted them, picking each one up for a kiss.

"Mommy's home," she told them. "Did you miss Mommy?"

Gina had only seen the dogs in photographs Nehra kept on her desk at work, but she had the same impression in person as she did of the pictures. They looked like little rodents.

"Paul," Tom said over the din. "You want a highball? I've got some good whiskey."

Paul rubbed his hands together.

Tom looked at Gina. "We also have wine."

"I'll have wine," she said. "Thank you."

Once the drinks were poured, the men went out to the yard to supervise the meat. Gina balanced on a barstool in the kitchen and watched Nehra clean and put away the things she had purchased at the market. She felt herself begin to relax. Surely, Mrs. Spark would take her duty seriously; she knew how important Ian was to her. If he needs me, she'll have him call here. She sipped her wine, listening to Nehra's chatter.

"There isn't anything you can't do when you're young, right?" Nehra stopped and pointed a knife at Gina. "You imagine you'll travel the world, then settle down. I have to tell you, I never had motherhood in me. I was thirty-one when we got married, still plenty of time, but it never seemed to be the *right* time. And then one day it was over and both of us seem to be fine with it."

"Is it?" Gina asked.

"What?"

"Is it over?"

"Gina, I'm forty this year."

She shrugged. "It's not so old anymore."

Nehra threw the bumpy skin of an avocado into the sink. "But weren't you listening? I never had motherhood in me, not once. And now, with all this Y2K stuff, it's a foolish time to bring a child into the world."

"Not you, too!"

"What?"

"Did you ever think maybe nothing will happen at all?"

Nehra shook her head vehemently. "Gina, it's nothing to joke about. You should be setting some things aside."

The men came back into the kitchen for refills on their drinks. Nehra made a point of looking at Tom when he reached around her for the whiskey bottle, but she didn't say anything.

"What about you, Paul?" Nehra asked. "Are you ready for Y2K?"

"No," he answered. "I don't think I am."

"Don't you worry about the stores running out of food and water? Some cars could be affected, they say."

"I've got an old car with nothing even remotely computer-like in it," Paul said. "As for food, I grow potatoes, corn, and some other things on a plot in my yard. I could survive better than most."

"You have enough room for corn?" she asked.

"Sure," he said. "I've got one row, turns out a good amount."

Gina finished her glass of wine. "I'd worry about my brother," she said. "The city would be the first place people would start acting like maniacs."

Nehra laughed. "What would you do, Gina? Drive downtown to save him?"

She blushed. "I might."

"Paul works downtown," Nehra said, looking ba[ck]

"I'm on Madison," he said. "That's where the [most]
of my time out and about though."

Tom came forward with the bottle of white

"Paul runs bike tours."

"City Bike Hikes," he said. "We do tours

She had seen the small groups of cyclists throughout the city. They always seemed ou[t] pedestrians, as though they had taken a exercise," she said.

He laughed, leaning his sharp elbo[w] like that, and the hours."

Nehra set a bowl of guacamole bag of tortilla chips. "Paul keeps a said. "And you're always reading, ri[ght]

"I do read, probably too mu[ch] about your job, Gina. Working f

"I'm a secretary."

Nehra put her hands on

'That must be interestin[g]

Gina took a big drink she didn't want to feel bad

Dinner was pleasan[t] avocado and fresh toma[to] work, of home. Paul li Berwyn by a success Concordia—and bo decades she'd bee northwest, while toward the city. Cabernet to ac Papers to file twenty-five the docume help Tom

dressin[g]
stacked

Gi[na]
bottle o[f]
tripped s[he]
from the
somehow,
crust in a
leaned agai[n]
reminded he[r]
the kitchen,
their glasses
into the living
and Nehra set
Paul.

And it cam[e]
business. Paul re
the nosy nurse, a
were they similar
where Paul was un[der]
Flushed, swea[t]
thought of her cord[ial]
already gone dead),
cleaning noises despit[e]
over, offered to get so
before Gina muttered
crashing into the coun[ter]
pressure in a loud, spl[it]
wreckage.

9

Through the fogged windows of Nehra's car, Gina stared at the treetops, the cedars and maples, poplars and pines, an orderly procession, a soft-edged frame. She fingered the small hole in the knee of her trousers; underneath, her skin burned and throbbed.

Nehra had fetched a bottle of rubbing alcohol and had made a fuss dabbing the knee with a moistened cotton ball. With one leg of her pants pulled up, Gina sat on the couch and bore it, the least she could do after breaking their coffee table and embarrassing everybody. Tom had been very gallant, insisting the table was old and needed to be replaced anyway. Nehra went so far as to thank Gina for doing away with it. And they all laughed, even Gina—inside, she burned.

After the accident, the night wound down rather quickly. Nehra offered to drive Paul and Gina home. Because Tom was too inebriated, she said. Silently, the threesome climbed into the car.

"You have to admit," Nehra said now, "it was a little funny."

Gina's eyes darted over in warning.

"I mean, you stumbled. Could have happened to anyone."

Gina looked out the window, avoiding Paul's eyes, which glistened from the depths of the back seat.

Nehra exhaled, her attempt at levity thwarted. They drove on in silence. Soon, they passed the expanse of a cemetery and Gina knew they were headed to Maywood to drop Paul first. She looked at the quiet streets, the town so like Berwyn with its brownstones, its golden streetlights, and mature trees. Soon, Nehra pulled up to a small house.

"Thanks," Paul said. "I'm sorry you have to drive all the way home. I should've brought my car."

"It's not far,' Nehra said. "And it's still early."

"Nice meeting you, Gina," he said. "I hope your knee is okay."

"It's fine," she said. "Have a good weekend, well, the rest of it."

He nodded.

They watched him walk to his door.

For a few miles, Nehra held her tongue. When they cleared the cemetery, she reached over and turned the radio down. "What about it, Gina? Will you help me get together a list for your anniversary party?"

"What?"

"Your twentieth. We want to do something at the office, you know, cake and all that business. I'll invite Ian and his wife, your lovely neighbor."

"Mrs. Spark?"

She looked over. "Yeah."

Gina closed her eyes. It was too much, all of it too much. She thought of Mrs. Spark, sitting on her worn chair with Gina's cordless telephone nearby as she cackled at her late-night reruns. "Let me think about it, Nehra. But really, it's not necessary."

They drove until eventually, Nehra turned onto the wider street that led to Gina's condo. A brief pause as she reloaded; Gina could feel it coming. "What did you think of Paul?" she asked.

"Seems nice," Gina said. "Only, I don't think you can hope for anything."

"Oh, I know." She laughed. "Did you see how much whiskey Tom drank?" She parked in a visitor space, turned off the engine, and followed Gina up to the door. Across the short distance between porches, Gina noticed a dim light from Mrs. Spark's kitchen. Nehra was right: it wasn't very late at all.

"Do you want to get your phone back?" Nehra asked.

"No, I have another one in the bedroom. I'll see her tomorrow."

"Can I come in for a minute? To tell you the truth, I'm irritated at Tom. Can't see why he has to throw back all that whiskey when he knows I'm serving wine. Let him sit with his headache for a while." She stopped, mid-step. "If that's okay with you." She shivered slightly in the purple dress despite the thick sweater she had thrown over it.

Gina turned the key in the lock and pushed the door. Once inside, Nehra took off her sweater and threw it over one of the dining room chairs.

"Do you want coffee?" Gina asked.

"Decaf?"

She nodded. At the cupboard next to the sink, she reached in for the can of Folgers, glancing at the tiny bottles of spirits, aligned in pleasing rows on the top shelf.

"You want to know who's really been pushing for a big party?" Nehra asked.

"Who?"

"Amanda."

"I'm sure it has nothing to do with me," Gina said. "She's trying to impress Mr. Seutter, but I don't think she has to worry about that."

Nehra's eyes widened.

Gina took two coffee mugs from the wooden holder on the wall. "She's pushy sometimes, that's all."

She thought about her mother, the way she flinched if someone was Standing Out, making a fuss at the grocery story, or speaking too loudly in a group. But in some way, she respected it, too. Gina knew this to be a fact because her sister, Deborah, was someone who could run a meeting, speak in front of a group, and even make quite a scene at the grocery store, if she wanted to. And yet their mother had admired Deborah.

"She's from a different generation, Gina. All that education. Do you ever think you should have gone to college? I think about it."

Gina pushed the button on the coffee maker and went to sit with Nehra. "I don't know."

"It wasn't really an option for me." Nehra looped her thumb through the purple belt and leaned back. "Thank goodness Tom got an education."

Gina thought about Ian and his curiosities. She always tied college to his inquisitiveness, thinking the only people really cut out for higher learning were the ones who were unsettled. She was content with the nightly news a few times a week, the occasional *Redbook* magazine. Through television and movies, she had travelled all over. She knew Italy from *Roman Holiday* and *Room with a View*, California more from *Chinatown* and *Irreconcilable Differences* than her few visits to Deborah in Sacramento. She had digested entire chunks of history by watching television miniseries: twentieth century Australia in *The Thorn Birds*, the Civil War in *North and South*.

She poured coffee for Nehra, half a cup for herself. She brought milk and sugar to the table.

Nehra took a sip and set the mug down gently. "My grandmother's sister stole a baby once," she said.

"What?"

She fussed with her hair, the coppery red sticking out between her fingers. "In China. This was many years ago, of course. She told everybody she was expecting. She wore loose clothing and seemed to gain weight in the right places.

No one suspected anything. She'd been married for a long time. Actually, it was overdue."

"I don't understand," Gina said.

"She pretended to be pregnant. When the time got close, whenever she had told them, she hired someone to drive her to a neighboring village. She stole a baby from one of the houses there and brought it back. Everyone celebrated."

"No one knew?"

Nehra shook her head. "It took a few months for the baby's family to find him."

"What happened?"

"They took him back. My grandmother's sister was considered crazy after that. She kept her husband but never had any children. It was a great embarrassment to my grandmother's family." She looked up. "Not the lack of children, the baby stealing."

"I'm sorry," Gina said.

She chuckled. "I didn't know her! I'm telling you people do crazy things."

Gina knew then the story had to do with what Mrs. Spark had told Nehra, about a daughter in California. The old woman probably told her everything in those few moments. The letters. That Michelle is a teacher. Damn Mrs. Spark.

She looked at Nehra. "I didn't know you were Chinese."

"I was born here."

"Yes, but—"

"Chinese mother, Czech and Polish father, an Englishman for a husband, and my mother gave me a name everyone thinks is Indian. I'm a walking United Nations." She reached across the table and touched Gina's arm, leaving her hand for several moments, until it became awkward. Both women straightened up and returned to the diversion of their coffee. They chatted a little about work, about Ian and his trip. Nehra suggested again that Gina get her phone back from Mrs. Spark, but Gina didn't want to see her. The interfering old woman surely would have made a fuss if Ian had called.

"I suppose I should get going," Nehra finally said.

Gina walked her to the door. She noticed a small hole in the armpit of Nehra's sweater as she put it on.

"I hope you had a little fun tonight," Nehra said.

"Oh, I did. Thanks for the dinner, for picking me up—"

"Enough of the mush," she said, giving Gina a gentle shove. "See you Monday." In the yellow light of the porch, she turned and looked back. "One of these days, Gina, you'll meet me halfway."

As she closed the door, Gina's mind was a tumult, not knowing what Nehra meant but not caring enough to linger on it, because it suddenly occurred to her that the condo was bone cold (and why hadn't Nehra said anything?). Also, she needed to get started on her nightly routines.

10
Berwyn, October 1978

The offices of Steadfast Insurance were above a noisy restaurant on Jackson Street. Each morning, Gina waded through the pungent medley of coffee, toasted bread, and fried breakfast meat, took the elevator to the fourth floor, and settled into the middle cubicle in a set of three. From her desk she could see mostly sky and a few buildings, but if she walked over and peered down, the plant-filled meridian splitting Jackson into northbound and southbound traffic jutted into the distance. To the right, the steel and glass of Sears Tower, surrounded by wisps of steam.

This day was dark, everything gray monochrome, a pregnant stillness in the sky. As though a thick layer of clouds had been condensed and pressed down. Nothing moving, no possibility of a storm and its release.

Gina hung her coat in the closet next to a small kitchen—really, a long strip of a room, with a counter and sink on one side and cupboards on the other—and settled into her desk. It had been months since the broker had left Steadfast. She'd heard he took a job at another agency for more pay. He never said goodbye. At first, she'd been disappointed, not realizing how much space the drama of his not talking to her had been taking up in her life. But soon she started to come back to herself and settle into a routine.

Sometimes she went for drinks after work with Bonnie and Linda, the two secretaries with desks on either side of hers. Bonnie was twenty-four like Gina and commuted from the suburbs, where she shared a house with two other girls. Linda was a bit older, twenty-eight and recently married, but her husband worked long hours at the stock exchange. At least once a week, they walked over to the blandly named *City Bar and Grill* for martinis and ham croquettes, or if they were ambitious and Linda had the entire evening, to a nicer restaurant for a full meal. She had plans with the girls that evening, a Thursday. Linda wanted to walk over to Berghoff's, an ancient but revered German restaurant in the south loop. Gina liked the food there but often, it was overcrowded, populated mostly with elderly patrons. Bonnie had suggested they have drinks down the street afterwards.

Gina went back to the kitchen for a cup of coffee—two packets of sugar, one centimeter of milk—and brought it to her desk. As she set it down, her telephone rang for the first time that day.

"Steadfast Insurance, Mr. Brine's office."

"Gina, is that you?" A woman's voice.

"Yes," she said, sipping her coffee.

"Sweetheart, it's Mrs. McDermott. Your neighbor."

Gina pressed the receiver against her ear. Thoughts fluttered by, something about insurance, something about the house?

"Hi, Mrs. McDermott." She pictured the older woman in the tight Bermuda shorts she wore in the summer, the paunch of her belly blooming underneath the high waist. They sometimes heard the McDermotts arguing, doors slamming.

"Gina, sweetheart. There's been an accident. Sweetheart, it's your daddy. He's been taken to the hospital."

"What?"

"You leave so early. I was waiting to call you. They've already gone to MacNeal."

MacNeal Hospital. "I don't understand," Gina said. "What happened?" Her father never left before 8:30; his office was only five-minutes away. What kind of accident could he have had at home?

Mrs. McDermott sucked in air. "I think it might have been a heart attack, sweetheart."

Gina looked around the office, which was slowly coming to life with arrivals and settling-ins. "What should I do?"

"Come home, sweetheart. I wish I could drive down and get you, but it's faster if you take a train."

"All right."

"I'll wait at the station. I'll head over in about a half-hour. You remember my car, the Dodge?"

"Yes."

Gina poured her coffee into the sink and got her coat. She left without speaking to anyone. In the lobby, Bonnie stood at the elevator door when it opened.

"Hey there, where are you going?"

From the restaurant, the smell of cooked bacon, hot grease, the dregs in a pot of coffee turning to syrup, all of it rushing in until Gina's stomach turned. "My father is in the hospital," she said. "Our neighbor called."

"Oh my God," Bonnie said, mouth open.

"Will you tell Mr. Brine?"

"Yeah, of course." She clutched the lapel of Gina's coat. "Call me."

The train ride, a terror of minutes stacked, one on top of the other. The empty seats made her feel like an outcast.

At her stop, Gina stepped down from the train and looked toward the small depot building. Squat and brick, like so many other buildings in Berwyn, the train station seemed slipshod and minimal, the quickest thing they could throw together to transition travelers from train to parking lot. She could see through the wide window next to the door, across the tiled vestibule, and through the opposite window into the parking lot, full of commuters' cars. When she pushed through the first door, she spotted Mrs. McDermott, the gray of the sky puffing up behind her, beyond the window but pressing down, framing everything, the coat buttoned high on the older woman's neck, so her head seemed to pop up, jack-in-the-box-like. As Gina walked closer and closer, across the tiles laid in an ornate pattern (one surprising flourish in the drab building), she remembered the night before when she had leaned over to kiss her father where he sat in his armchair, head lowered to a *Scientific American*, something about conduits on the page, with a diagram of electrical pathways signified in purple and blue, like veins, like rivers, and the smell of his cologne lingering underneath the residue of the day: sweat, food, cigarette smoke—not his but someone he must have seen in his office—all of it a rapid missile delivered to her senses when she, thoughtlessly, routinely, bent down to kiss his cheek. As she neared Mrs. McDermott and saw her blanched face, the things Gina remembered and the things she knew started to dissolve together and if she could fully articulate anything at that moment, with the clouds pressing down and then, the pressure of Mrs. McDermott's plump arm around her shoulders, it was the sense that the goodnight kiss would be something she would never forget, no matter what happened.

The funeral was four days later. They stood in a single line at the gravesite, Helen clutching Ian's arm. He was getting tall, in the midst of one last phase of thinness before he'd grow chubby again and for good. Deborah came from California and brought Dan, her boyfriend from college, although Dan had dropped out to run his father's carpet-cleaning business. Gina thought their father would have been disappointed, having always expected lofty things for Deborah.

Aunt Klara flew in from Atlanta. Uncle Pete was unable to get away from work, she said, but they all knew the money for his plane ticket was probably an issue. Always scraping by, Helen often said about her only sister. Their cousin Roxana, Klara's daughter, was married already and had recently delivered her first baby, a boy. Aunt Klara waited until later that night, after the visitors and the food, the constant pacing and murmuring, after Ian was asleep and Helen had finally agreed to lie down, to bring out photos of her new grandson.

They sat in the living room—Deborah, Dan, Gina, and Aunt Klara.

"Look at that," she said, passing the photo. "He's got your Uncle Pete's fat toes." Aunt Klara had grown softer since the last time Gina had seen her. Her middle had spread to the width of the rest of her body; her face was accented with tiny wrinkles. When she walked into the church that afternoon, Gina's first thought was how much her aunt had come to resemble Grandma Sahlin, a pin prick amidst the rest of the pain.

Deborah squinted at the photograph in the dim light. "How can you tell?"

"Maybe the picture is too small," Aunt Klara said.

"Cute," Dan said. He handed the tiny square to Gina and laced his fingers through Deborah's. Gina noticed it then: the small, diamond ring on her sister's left hand. She looked at the baby's photo. Fat face, blue jumpsuit. Nothing to look at.

"How's your job, Deborah?" Aunt Klara asked. "You're working in admissions?"

"Yes." Deborah glanced at Dan. "It's like I'm still in college, in a way."

"When's the wedding?" Gina asked.

Her sister's mouth tightened. "We haven't said anything. We thought it would be better to wait."

"What?" Aunt Klara rose from her chair. "Deborah? Oh, that's wonderful, really wonderful." She crossed the room, hugged her niece and admired the ring.

Gina looked away, towards the stairs, hoping that Ian and her mother were sleeping at last. She needed a break from the heaviness of their grief and uncertainty. The way their eyes kept meeting hers, welling up, looking away. But not this, not Deborah elated.

Aunt Klara sat back down. "I think it's delightful, really. This will be welcome news, believe me. Your mother has a romantic heart, underneath it all."

They sat quietly for a few moments, the kitchen clock clunking in painful little jabs.

"I'm going to tell you a story," Aunt Klara said. "About your parents."

Gina closed her eyes, knowing she couldn't stop her, didn't have the strength. Whatever the story was, she didn't want to hear it.

"When your father was young, he looked like a movie star. Let's face it, girls, and we keep this to ourselves: your father was a very attractive older man, too."

Deborah shook her head. "Come on, Aunt Klara, that's weird."

"You'll realize that someday." She brought her feet up and crossed her legs, like some well-dressed sage. "He was very romantic. Your mother met him at a party."

Deborah leaned forward. "Her friend's birthday, right?"

She nodded. "Henry was a cousin of one of the girls, visiting from Decatur. Dragged along to the party, even though he was a couple of years older." She smiled. "Helena was smitten right away, came home talking up a storm about him."

"And for years, they wrote letters," Gina said quickly, "and then he came up to attend Northern Illinois and they met again." The whole thing was bothering her, Aunt Klara speaking about her father in his own house, making *their* story her own.

"Gina," Deborah said. "Let her tell it."

"I'm sorry," Aunt Klara said. "I know you girls knew your daddy. I was remembering how romantic he was. Sent Helena flowers all the time, wrote her tender letters. And they both could be quite jealous."

"Jealous?" Deborah sputtered. "I can't imagine that."

Aunt Klara nodded, lowered her voice. "Do you remember that time we went to Wisconsin?"

Deborah explained to Dan, "We rented a cabin once, before Ian was born. I think I was about ten years old."

"There was a family at the campsite," their aunt said. "We had cookouts with them."

"They were sort of hippies," Deborah said.

She nodded. "The Taggerts. I don't know why I remember their names, but I do. Dawn and John. Funny, right? Well, over the course of the week, Dawn Taggert became flirtatious with your father."

"With Daddy?" Deborah said.

"This is what I'm telling you." Aunt Klara's eyes widened. "About your father. And about your mother. Helena was so mad, but I think part of her appreciated that he could appeal to someone else."

Deborah lowered her face onto her hands, her shoulders shaking. Dan put his arm around her.

Gina's grief became a live thing, expanding, squeezing everything out. She focused on controlling her vocal chords, on keeping her feet still. Tears fell but she wouldn't allow herself to rant and rave, to Stand Out. Not here, not now. In a low voice, she said, "She wants to be called Helen."

Aunt Klara reached for a nearby box of tissue and blew her nose. As she wiped and patted around her nostrils, the stairs creaked, and they all turned.

Hair mussed, pajamas buttoned up the wrong way, with one side hanging lower than the other, Ian stood on the bottom step, his forehead crinkled and a look of sleepy confusion on his face.

At first Gina thought he was sleepwalking because of the way his eyes avoiding lingering on anything. His hands were two pasty fists at his sides. He remained on the stair, suspended between the realm of grief they were building below and the refuge above, looking from one wet face to another. "What happened?" he asked.

And Gina sprung up, rushing around the chair, over the thick carpet to reach him, support him, before he suddenly remembered.

11

Gina was in the hall bathroom of her condo, leaning her head against the wall behind the toilet. She exhaled, trying to remember if she had used Nehra's restroom even one time, in the three hours or so she had been there. Too much wine. She tensed at the memory of falling through the coffee table. The awkward comments, the stricken faces. Nehra had laughed outright, in the way people can when someone gets hurt. But quickly, she had become the adept hostess, with rubbing alcohol, the right words, and attempts to rebalance the mood.

Gina opened her eyes and looked around. She had left the door open, but the only view was the wall opposite, shadowed and bare. Next to the door, the beige hand towels with their scrolled green design, lined up on the chrome rod, the end one slightly crooked and rumpled. On the sink, the soap in its ivory dish, small and pink and scalloped like a shell, sitting in a puddle of water. Next to that, a brown leather wallet.

An alarm sounded and Gina started. She sat completely still. Another ringing, a bell. The doorbell. She looked at her watch: 10:14.

She rolled a swatch of toilet paper around her hand and finished up. It could be Nehra. Mrs. Spark? Ian? This last thought, however improbable, hurried her along, the idea that her brother could have come back early, maybe without Carrie, maybe having decided the whole thing was a big mistake and needing her now to pick up the pieces.

At the door, she looked through the peephole and the compressed, distorted image made no sense at all. Still, her head swam a bit from the wine and the fall, and maybe her heart needed a rest. She turned the handle.

Tall and dark, hair slicked back like glistening strings of licorice, he had backed onto the second step after ringing the bell. "Hello again."

Without intending to, she moved slightly behind the door. "Paul?"

He pushed his hands further into the pockets of his coat, beige and rough-looking, with matted wool around the collar. "I hope it's not too late. I don't mean to disturb."

She shivered a bit, moved one arm across her chest. "It's colder."

He looked up at the sky. "Smells like rain. I guess we're not through with it yet."

"Well, why don't you come in?" Gina said, because it was the thing to say.

Before she could take a breath, Paul was at her side, past her in a breeze of earthy smells, towering in the living room.

"When we stopped by earlier," he said, "I left my wallet here."

"Oh," she said. "Yes."

He made a move towards the hall, but Gina blocked his path. "I can get it for you."

"Yes," he said, stepping back. "Thank you."

She flew down the hall, grabbed the wallet and shut the bathroom door behind her. When she came back out, Paul was sitting at the table. She put the wallet down in front of him.

"Thanks," he said again.

She stood at the entrance to the kitchen, noticing now the answering machine and its bright red zero. No messages. She glanced towards the cupboard, thinking of having a nightcap but after the episode at Nehra's, this would certainly give the wrong impression. But why should she care what this man thinks?

As if reading her mind, he said, "I don't suppose you have any gin?"

Gina went to the cupboard. "No gin," she said. "But I have vodka. Absolut."

He nodded, an encouraging look on his face.

"I like it with club soda," she said. "But I'm out. Orange juice?"

"A screwdriver," he said. "Perfect."

She mixed the drinks slowly, careful of her nervous hands. Her back was turned, but when she heard the chair creak and scrape along the floor, she looked over and he was taking off his coat. Underneath, the checked shirt he had worn to dinner: tiny, worn blue squares on a field of white.

When she brought the drinks, she passed the plant on the counter. What had he called it? Firecracker something? "So, you like plants?" she asked.

He clinked his glass against hers and motioned for her to sit on the chair closest to him. He took a long drink. "I do," he said. "I think Nehra told you I have a small garden, a bit of landscaping. What about you?"

She swallowed the liquid she'd been swirling around her tongue. Sweet, metallic, slightly bitter. "No, I can't keep plants alive. Once in a while, I'll buy something for the kitchen but forget to water it."

"Me and plants get along," he said. "I don't know why. They have simple needs."

"I'm hungry," Gina said. Normally, she'd be taken aback to have said such a thing out loud to someone she barely knew, but at some point, something inside of her had let go. She didn't give two shakes what this man thought of her, and it had been a very, very long day.

His hand moved slightly towards hers. "What do you have?"

She rose and went to the freezer. Moving around the boxes, she pulled one out. "Apple strudel," she said. "It's frozen, but heated in the microwave, with a scoop of ice cream—"

"Oh, those are great," he said. "Have you tried the molten lava cake?"

"No, good?" Gina opened the box and pushed the right buttons.

"Very," he said. "The single life."

"What?"

"When you live alone, you appreciate the frozen stuff, dinners for one."

"I don't cook anymore," she said.

"Hardly worth it to cook for one person," he said. "Tonight was a treat for me, at Nehra and Tom's."

Gina walked to the table and had a drink from her glass.

"I was married once." Paul scratched his chin, the nails finding the stubble there with a papery sound. "My ex-wife lives in Oregon, took a trip there when we were still married and loved it. Loves the trees, she says, even likes the rain. I haven't talked to her for a couple of years now."

The microwave beeped. "I've never been married." Gina scooped the strudel into bowls and added the ice cream. At the table, they ate for a few moments without speaking.

"Where's your family from?" he asked.

"Around here," she said. "My grandmother was Swedish. Have you ever had Swedish food? She used to make this meat pie—minced beef, cabbage, baked in a pocket of bread. You could never find that in the frozen aisle."

"Sounds like a runza."

"A what?"

"Something *my* grandma used to make," he said. "She was German, though. Her family lived for years in Nebraska, but she came here with my grandpa."

"Can you imagine uprooting your whole life?"

Paul smiled. "When I was younger and more romantic, maybe. Now, I don't know. You get pretty settled, don't you?"

They finished their drinks.

"Want another?" he asked. "I'll make them."

As Gina watched, he got up and moved comfortably around the kitchen. "Did you get the recipes from your Swedish grandmother?" he asked.

"No," she said. "My mom never made any of it. I don't know whether my grandma didn't teach her, or she didn't want to learn." She dug the last bit of melted ice cream from the sides of her bowl, licking her spoon. "They had a strained relationship, I guess."

"Listen," Paul said. "I grew up with three sisters. All relationships between women in a family are strained."

She reached up and took the fresh drink from him. "I don't know about that."

"Don't be offended," he laughed. "You know it's true. Relationships between men aren't any easier, only different."

Gina thought about the times they went to her grandmother's, the rift that seemed to open between her mother and the older woman. But relationships viewed from the outside were only the tip of the iceberg. The conversations at the table over kaffe, her mother's strained expressions, her grandmother's interfering. The relationship Gina saw was a small, small portion of what was between them. What would someone think, Gina wondered, when viewing the particulars of her and Deborah's relationship—the infrequent phone calls, the snappy comments, the things left out? From the outside, someone might think they weren't close at all, but a cursory view doesn't show anything at all, doesn't show the childhood games and the understandings, the entire debris of growing up with the same parents in the same house. Their grown-up lives might not intersect too often, but that shared past was a huge thing, like an underground system of caves and tunnels, larger than the house itself.

"Wow," she said. "Three sisters."

Lines came out along the side of his mouth. "I had a brother, too, but he's gone. My sisters live around here. All of them married, with kids. They mother me a bit, you know, because I'm the youngest. Seems funny to get mothered at forty-six years old. But they've always been there." He looked at her across the table. Despite the few, deep lines on his brow and the occasional gray hair along his temples, there was something boyish about him. "The middle one, Lorraine, is probably closest to me," he said. "We see things the same way most of the time. She's down in La Grange, not too far. She's got two boys, fifth and sixth grade.

My parents are in La Grange, too. Retired, of course, slowing down. Lorraine watches over them."

The warmth from the drink, from the apple paste of the strudel, was spreading through her. Gina settled into the chair.

"Your parents?" he asked.

She shook her head. "My mother died three years ago. Cancer."

"She was pretty young?" he asked.

Gina looked up, startled by the question, because her mother had lived so much longer than her father. "Sixty-four," she said.

He made a soft blowing sound. "That's tough. Sorry." His hand circled the glass. "Is your father still here?"

As she shook her head, a glaring truth came to her, something she had never thought about much. "My father was forty-seven—"

Paul looked up, his eyes behind the lenses catching the overhead light.

"—when he died," she finished. "He had a heart attack. One day, everything was normal and the next, he was gone. Like he left on a trip."

His hand shot across the table, covered hers. "Damn, Gina. That's rough, really rough."

Not now. You're tired. Such a long day.

"He was my age," Paul said. "Think of that." He patted her hand; like electric shocks, the contact spread up her arm. "Oh, you're crying," he said.

Suddenly, he was standing behind her, his tall frame bent awkwardly, his long arms reaching around to embrace her, one hand on each shoulder, the hair on his arms tickling her chin, his cheek resting briefly on her head. "Let's go sit over there," he said, guiding her out of the chair with his hands, turning her towards him but instead of moving towards the living room, their bodies pressed together.

He was tall, so tall. His arms, one over the other, a large X across her back. Her face against the soft checked shirt with its translucent buttons, taking in his smell. Paul patted her lower back with warm hands, the gesture so soothing she couldn't bring herself to move, even as she was aware of the moment and its impropriety and the uncomfortable moments that were sure to follow, and her breasts pressed against the soft cushion of his stomach, his belt seeming to brace them and below that, something insistent against her abdomen.

His breathing, tattered, his hands coming up now, tangled in her hair, pulling her head back to face him. Her legs faltered and he brought an arm around her waist, steadying her. They walked towards the couch, and he directed her onto the cushion and lowered himself down. Suddenly, they were at an even level, his face close to hers and she gave up and fell back against the couch, letting her legs relax.

He pressed his mouth to her neck, his hand flat against the triangle of flesh exposed at the opening of her shirt. She didn't know what to do with her own hands at first and they flailed, fishlike, on the couch, then slowly, went to his shoulders. He moved to the other side of her neck, and she had a fleeting thought he was avoiding her face. His hand moved down to her breast, and his stubbly chin irritated the soft skin of her neck. Then, his face reappeared as he moved in to kiss her.

It was all there: the earthiness, the strudel, the faint tang of orange. She was relieved when he moved away, when his mouth continued on, and nothing was required of her. She became aware of a small movement, a vibration, almost tied to a sound, something internal. Distracting. Half of her blouse was unbuttoned; her hands were gripping Paul's shoulders and she looked up to see them, acting with their own intent.

The vibration again, rattling. She realized it was her legs, shaking. Suddenly, his hands left her breasts and came around, pulling her to a sitting position against his body. He nuzzled his face into her hair and held her, her body relaxing into his and her arms fully around his lean shoulders now, pulling him closer.

"Gina?" A small voice, followed by a rapping on the door.

Paul bolted upright, dropping her against the cushions.

They both looked towards the door.

"Gina. It's me, Madge. I've got your phone."

Gina's hands went to her throat, her chest, the open buttons needing to be closed. She pressed her knees together and pushed herself upright. Paul moved to the edge of the couch.

"Gina!" The old woman's voice rose.

Paul stood up, held out his hand. He pulled her up from the couch and quickly, she removed her hand from his grasp. Too quickly. He looked away and she felt instantly remorseful. What was she doing?

The door was white and when Gina opened it, the outside pressed forward in a widening screen, outlined in black—distant cars, crickets, the jangling colors of Mrs. Spark's shirt, her silver car parked in front, all of it illuminated by the shrill porch light.

A tangle of grayish hairs rose above each of Mrs. Spark's rheumy eyes. "Why, Gina. You're flushed."

Stretched to full extension, the door squeaked from the hinges. Mrs. Spark's eyes traveled to Paul, who had stepped forward.

"Hello again," he said.

The old woman looked back and forth between them. "Sure is cold out here."

Gina sighed and stepped backwards.

Mrs. Spark limped towards Paul. She could act like a regular old lady when she wanted to. "Never rang all night," she said, lifting the phone up. "I checked the dial tone, every hour. It's definitely working."

Under Mrs. Spark's faded plaid coat, Gina noticed the blue seam of the tee shirt underneath. Her *Pepsi Generation* shirt, Gina realized, and when she thought about the fact that Mrs. Spark often wore a *Coke is Life* shirt, a slow stew of anger began to bubble. Because really, didn't the old woman care at all about Not Standing Out, about how she appeared to people?

Paul cleared his throat. "It was nice of you to keep it."

"Yes, Mrs. Spark." Gina held out her hand. "Thank you."

But the old woman wasn't finished yet, wasn't ready to relinquish her participation in the evening. She looked away and kept the phone gripped tightly. "How was your dinner?" she asked Paul.

He glanced at Gina. "The brisket was cooked perfectly. Too much food for me, probably." His hands went to his stomach, which was flat as a board, but he patted it anyway.

Gina wished he would stop.

"You gotta live," Mrs. Spark chirped.

The cold was fully in the condo now, the door having been left open. Gina started to say "It's late" at the same moment Mrs. Spark spoke again.

"You'll never guess what I saw tonight."

Paul crossed his arms and settled back on his heels. Gina had the distinct impression he was amused and wouldn't be helping her get rid of her neighbor.

Mrs. Spark tottered on her feet, waiting, no doubt, for Gina to offer her a seat. "I was flipping through my movie channels, you know how I do."

Another look from Paul at this, but Gina kept her eyes on the old woman.

"And I got distracted by this one movie and ended up watching most of it. The woman was beautiful, with big, blue eyes, although she dressed mannish sometimes."

"Mrs. Spark," Gina said, shivering.

"And she was a Marine, this woman, so that made her tough, you see? She gets a job at this school for bad kids, the ones who can't put two and two together. They'd rather be out causing trouble."

Paul nodded. "I think I know that movie."

"The kids really give her a hard time, but then they get to know her. And do you know what that actress's name was, her real name?"

The room became a stifling place, despite the cool air from outside. Gina wanted to take the phone from Mrs. Spark's hand and crack her skull with it. "It's getting late," she said.

"Her name was Michelle!" The old woman was triumphant, the silver hair under the kerchief glimmering, her colorless lips spreading, her voice strong and sure. "Like your daughter, Gina. It was like everything you told me. She's a teacher, too, and that student, the one with the problem—"

"*Dangerous Minds*," Paul said. "That's the name of it."

Suddenly, the phone in Mrs. Spark's hand emitted a faint sound, like a wounded version of its usual ring. From the bedroom, the other phone echoed.

In a flurry of moments, Gina seized the phone, threw Paul's coat to him, and shooed them out of the house. "It's Ian," she said, over and over in the rush, in her panic. "Long distance. It's Ian."

She left them standing on the porch. The last thing she saw was Paul leaning down to take Mrs. Spark's arm and her upturned, wizened face, smiling broadly.

And Gina hoped the telephone had enough strength remaining to connect her to her lost brother, as she pushed the green button and with trembling hands, held the receiver to her ear. Nothing. She raced down the hallway and into her bedroom, noticed the strong light from the other telephone, the fully charged one.

"Ian," she sputtered as she lunged for it. "Ian?"

"As they proceeded there, black wings thudded in sudden unison, and a flock of birds flew up as they might from a ploughed field, still shaped like it, like an old map that still served new territory, and wrinkled away in the air."

— Eudora Welty, *The Optimist's Daughter*

Flight

12

Hear the winding, rushing sounds of an airport: jets exhaling, the high whir of the engines with background bass hum, wheeled suitcases scraping along concrete. Automobiles shoot bursts of sun to the terminal windows; warped, undulating versions are reflected back. Couples cling in long embraces next to cars parked at angles in the drop-off zone. Along the narrow pathways, sole travelers, stooped against the cold and isolation, hurry along. The smells are toxic, non-human: car exhaust, damp metal, processed food.

On one of those pathways, a woman in a long coat rifles through her handbag and retrieves a tissue, which she presses first to her upper lip, then her forehead. Near her feet, an upright suitcase waits like an obedient child. Her hair is combed down, and a few stray bangs fall across her wide forehead.

From a distance, the woman is another face in the crowd, another traveler pausing for breath. But if she were a friend, a sister, you'd be able to tell that the day is not a typical one, not for Gina S.

Gina had never left her new car outside of her care and even now, a vision of its silver-blue shell, surrounded by the other abandoned vehicles in long-term parking, pulled at her. She had never travelled outside the country before, and her heart was thumping.

Inside the airport, she absorbed the echo of voices and cold whoosh of air, the white and metal surfaces bringing to mind Ian's igloo in Proksa Park, his glittering eyes, his joy. The line was long. She stood behind a woman who seemed to be traveling for business. In one hand, a shiny leather briefcase, the other resting on the extended handle of her suitcase, which matched Gina's in size and shape but seemed so much smarter.

Gina wore her sturdy shoes, in navy blue, with pants of the same color. She had tried on one shirt after another, all of them button-up, all versions of the same thing in different hues. She had chosen one in light blue and in a rush of inspiration, had climbed up on the wooden chair in her room and found at the back of her closet a sweater she had purchased but never worn. White and remarkably soft, possibly an impractical choice. But it would keep her warm on the airplane because it covered her neck and the area exposed below that. Reddening, she remembered the night before, Paul's scalp visible beneath his dark hair as he burrowed into her chest.

The line moved forward slowly. There were three women working United's check-in desk, all her age or older, each wearing the same, creased uniform and haggard expression she remembered from every time she'd ever travelled. The last trip was three years ago, the visit to her sister's. Her nephew's football game, where Deborah's friends asked a few, introductory questions then ignored her, chatting about their nail appointments and house renovations, their hapless babysitters and hopeless husbands. This last part they whispered because the husbands were there, pacing up and down the sidelines.

Deborah. She should have called her, no matter the time. What if something happened?

"Next in line."

Gina walked to the counter and handed the woman her driver's license. "My brother made the reservation on the phone," she said. "Last night."

The woman swung her heavily outlined eyes towards the computer and punched several keys.

"I don't have a ticket," Gina said. "But I have a confirmation number."

"I have it," the woman said. "Checking bags?"

"I'm sorry?"

"Do you have any luggage?"

She reached over, gripped the handle.

"No, leave it for now," the woman snapped. "How many?"

Flustered, Gina let go. "Just one."

"Your passport?"

"Oh, yes."

She remembered standing in line at the federal building, her photos and paperwork in hand, thinking about sunsets in Greece. A trip she had planned with coworkers but in the end, she had cancelled. Placing the small, blue folder with its gold-stamped insignia on the counter, she felt a twinge of competence.

The woman looked it over and raised her eyes. "First time using it, hon?"

Gina nodded.

Something had softened on the woman's face. She handed back the passport, the license, and two green and white boarding passes. "You'll have to change planes in Tokyo. Looks like you have two hours. Plenty of time."

"Will anything be in English?" she asked. "I mean, the signs?"

"I've made a special mark on your reservation," the woman said. "The flight attendants will be looking out for you. Can you lift your bag onto the platform now?"

Looking out for me, Gina thought. Half of her was offended and the other half relieved. She watched as her suitcase was carried away on the conveyer belt. Her purse felt suddenly light and easy to manage.

"Gate 17B," the woman said. "This way to security."

Gina's eyes followed the direction of the pointed finger to an open area, another long line. "Thank you," she said.

She found her gate without incident and boarded the plane when her section was called. Her window seat was on the right side, her view blocked by the wing. One of the less preferred seats for this reason, she assumed, and probably one of the few left when Ian called last night, on short notice. She wondered what the ticket had cost him. Round trip, all the way to Seoul. She couldn't imagine.

A short, balding man hurried down the aisle, looking in her direction. Gina glanced at the two seats still empty next to her. He stopped and stood on his toes to push a compact black bag into the overhead compartment. Giving her a slight nod, he ducked into the aisle seat. The first leg of the trip was almost thirteen hours. If the middle seat remained empty, they'd have much more room.

Her eyes were dry, the pressurized air in the cabin making them drier. She took off her glasses and closed them, remembering the conversation with Ian the night before.

On the long-distance call, his voice had been familiar but strange at the same time. "Gina? Gina, are you there?"

"Ian!" Her voice cracked as she sat on the edge of the bed, concentrating every cell on hearing him.

"There you are," he said. "I called yesterday."

"I was still on the train. You didn't leave a number."

"It's a pay phone." Other sounds came forward now: traffic, wind, voices. "I'm so glad I got you this time."

"Ian, I've been worried."

"Gina, please don't ask a lot of questions. Just listen."

The tone of his voice caused her back to straighten.

"I need you to come here," he said. "Tomorrow. I called the airline and found a flight that leaves at 10:15 in the morning. O'Hare airport to Gimpo International, through Tokyo. It's about seventeen hours total, two hours layover.

I'll pick you up. We rented a car." A woman's voice in the background. "Carrie says hi."

"I don't understand," Gina said. "What's happening?"

"The short version," Ian said, "is we need you here to finalize the adoption. Please trust me. This is everything to me, to us. I'll explain when you get here."

"But I have to work on Monday." Her head was spinning. She wasn't even sure where Korea was.

"He'll understand," Ian said. "You never take time off."

"When would I come back?"

"I'm hoping by Wednesday," he said. "You won't arrive until five o'clock Monday evening, so we won't get anything done that day."

"What do you mean?"

Ian sighed, and the background noise grew muffled. She realized he had put his hand over the receiver.

"Okay," he said. "Remember that night we came over and you signed a few papers, things pertaining to getting Hana?"

She nodded, then said quickly, "Yes."

"One of those was an agreement to be a guardian, sort of a back-up in case anything happens to either of us."

Gina didn't recall anything like that but didn't want Ian to think she signed the papers without reading them. But he had never mentioned it, either.

"And because of some, well, some complications, they want to see you. Normally, that doesn't happen."

"What complications?"

"Gina, please. We'll have lots of time to explain everything."

She pictured him, standing on some street corner, cars puttering by on a dirt road, Carrie clinging to his arm. Fruit sellers with wooden carts, people in funny hats—really, she had no idea how to picture a Korean street, so the images behind and around him were vague but the main thing was Ian's face, his pleading eyes, the hint of a smile.

"Tell me what to do," she said.

She found her passport in the safe, pulled her suitcase from the closet and packed most of it before she collapsed into bed near one o'clock. At six, her alarm clock buzzed. She left a voicemail message on Mr. Seutter's phone and another on Nehra's work line. She wrote a note for Mrs. Spark, asking her to keep an eye on the condo for a few days. Then she showered and drove to the airport.

13
Berwyn, June 1995.

Gina pulled up to the condo in her Honda Accord and turned the key back. The engine made a cranky sound before quitting, a sharp noise she was trying not to think about since she had recently signed the daunting papers of her first mortgage and couldn't consider another expense.

From the trunk she retrieved two, green-shaded lamps, a gift from her mother. She juggled them, her purse, and her newly bulkier key ring as she walked to the door. The moving truck would be arriving within the hour. Gina had left the three workers at the brownstone, where they'd been struggling with her mattress in the curvy entryway.

She unlocked the door of the condo and set down the lamps on the kitchen counter. The doorbell rang.

On the porch, an elderly woman in a *California Girl* tee-shirt stood with a cellophane-wrapped plate. "Welcome, neighbor!" she said with a gravelly voice.

"Hello." Gina let the door open wider.

"I saw you here the other day. Moving in, are you?"

"Yes, today." She stepped back. "Would you like to come in?"

The woman was past Gina and into the living room before the screen door shut. She maneuvered much more quickly than her hunched frame and aging face implied.

"I'm Madge Spark," she said. "I brought you cookies, not homemade. I don't bake anymore." She looked around. "This is like my condo."

"Is it?"

"Exactly." She thrust the plate towards Gina. "Have a cookie."

"Sorry, I don't have any plates, nothing to drink, nowhere to sit."

The old woman laughed. "No, you don't, do you? Come to my place. You're Gina, right?"

"Yes, but how—"

A wave of her arm. "The cable company left a card on your doorknob. I have it at my apartment. It could have blown away."

"Oh, thank you," she said. "I think they're0 coming tomorrow?"

Mrs. Spark leaned forward, until Gina could smell her fusty breath. "Well, I didn't *read* it!"

They crossed the small distance between their homes, and Gina was treated to the first of what would be many tours of the front porch. Mrs. Spark told her the crèche had been the initial component of her display, a holiday gift from her son when he got his first job. She liked the Virgin Mary to stand outside the stable, she said, to see what might be coming next.

There was Popeye, the stone animals, and two eyeless geese almost lost in the confused scene. The geese were to the side of the front door, and Gina tripped on them that first day and almost every other time afterwards. There was the leprechaun with his gray beard and the matching, lighted buckles on his hat and belt. A rainbow balanced between his upturned palms, even then flickering a bit.

What wasn't explained on that tour, or on any of the subsequent ones Gina would have, was *why* Mrs. Spark kept the items on her porch, especially the seasonal ones, even on a June day, when it probably increased her electricity bill and especially when it made the entire porch cluttered and virtually unusable. After the first Christmas had passed and the animals and characters stayed on the porch, after Gina and Mrs. Spark had had many conversations about her son and Gina's brother, about Mrs. Spark's television shows and Gina's job, after all the time being neighbors, the time for asking had passed.

That first afternoon, they talked in Mrs. Spark's dark kitchen, which was also cluttered with things that belonged elsewhere. Along one wall, shoeboxes were stacked, and an old sewing machine was pushed into a corner. Mrs. Spark took a long time making two mugs of instant coffee. Finally sitting at the kitchen table, she brought forth a photograph. "I have a son," she said, setting it down.

Gina looked at the picture. A middle-aged man, balding but vigorous, his arm around a blonde woman with great teeth. In the front, a boy of about ten, down on one knee next to a soccer ball and a smaller girl, clutching her mother's hand. "They're—" she started.

"He hardly comes to visit," Mrs. Spark interrupted. "He's an engineer at Ford, seven people working under him."

"That's nice," she said. "We had a Ford when I was young, although I can't remember the name of it. Maybe Falcoln?"

"I don't understand it," she said. "How can a son forget his mother?"

Gina, feeling awkward, stirred her coffee with the tarnished spoon.

"His wife's a piece of work. Stays home but still has those children in daycare after school. What she does all day, I'd like to know. She can't cook, that's a fact."

"What's his name?" Gina asked.

Mrs. Spark's head popped up. "Who?"

"Your son."

"Howard Jr. The little girl is Kate, and the boy is Treat. Couldn't be Howard the third like my dear husband would have wanted."

(Gina found out later that the grandson's name was Trent.) "Where do they live?" she asked.

"In Oak Park." Mrs. Spark leaned forward. "Their neighbors on both sides are Chinese!"

Gina nodded. In earlier years, Berwyn and neighboring towns like Oak Park were peopled with descendants of Czechs, Poles, Ukrainians, Swedes like Gina's family. Gina had no reason to be prejudiced against the Hispanic, Black and Asian families she saw everywhere now, but she did notice the difference. There couldn't be anything wrong with *noticing*.

Mrs. Spark dunked her cookie in the lukewarm coffee. "He's a big baby, that's what he is."

Gina strained her ears for the moving truck.

"You should see him." Her lips curled around the mug's rim as she took a noisy sip. "When he does come over, he lies on that couch like the Queen of Sheba and wants me to fix him something to eat. He gripes about his job. He has responsibility, but it's not difficult labor like his father did. Most sickness is in the head now. Used to be, you'd have a backache at the end of the day, but it was honest work. Now, my son's worried about taking a trip next year or putting that little girl in math classes, before she's even in Kindergarten!" She took a soggy bite and crumbs flew when she finished, "Do a hard day's work, that's what I say to him."

Gina finished her coffee, which was bitter and cooling. She scooted her chair back.

"Does your family ever disappoint you, Gina?"

She looked at the old woman. "What?"

Mrs. Spark leaned forward. "Are you ever disappointed in your family? We only get one, no returning them for a newer model."

Gina thought first of Ian. They still had Wednesday dinners at their mother's, although recently it was take-out because Helen didn't seem to have energy for cooking. Going to a movie or a football game with her brother had become a rare event, and he didn't call her as much anymore. There had been other times throughout their lives when they'd grown a bit distant, but they had always weathered through it. When their father died, Gina was twenty-four and Ian was thirteen. The ensuing years were probably Ian's most difficult, but they weren't that bad. He grew his hair longer and plastered his room with posters of bands. He became obsessed with real-life pirates then studied the Civil War for months, and maybe he didn't open up to Gina as much during those years. He made a neighborhood friend, and the two boys would hole up in Ian's room for hours when she thought they'd be better off outside, getting fresh air. At sixteen, Ian got a job at a local pizza place and paid back some of the money Helen had fronted for his car. Gina remembered the dented, red hatchback, the glass prism that hung from the rear-view mirror, throwing shards of color, and almost blinding her any time she rode with him. But even through those times of transition and occasional awkwardness, her brother was always kind.

But disappointed? Gina could never feel anything close to disappointment where Ian was concerned. With Deborah? Mostly regret and a mild sadness. Her mother? A question mark. Her father?

"No," she said. "I've never been disappointed."

Mrs. Spark clucked her tongue. "You're lucky."

A strange thing happened then. Gina looked at Mrs. Spark's *California Girl* tee shirt and the untidy kitchen. The instant coffee coated her tongue with its deplorable badness. And something about the old woman's tone, the way she seemed to sit in judgment of Gina or maybe wish disappointment on her, something about this ignited a wick of twined resentment and let loose an impulse that normally Gina would have quieted, as she did when Amanda Blevin said things like "Oh, I forgot you've been working here *so* long," as though Amanda's life was a fabulous string of adventures, a floating raft down a river where Gina sat like a toad on a stump; something about Mrs. Spark's hostility, which certainly couldn't be reasonably aimed at Gina, whom she had known so briefly, but which still stung in ways that were familiar, this antipathy, this dismissal, over what should have been a neighborly plate of cookies; Mrs. Spark's statement about luck unearthed something.

"I have a daughter," Gina said.

The old woman's head rose in interest.

"She lives in California."

Mrs. Spark nodded her approval.

"Her name is Michelle. She's a teacher of disadvantaged kids."

"What does that mean?"

Gina waved her hand. "You know, children from poor areas, sometimes from broken homes."

The old woman gave another frugal nod.

"She teaches ninth grade. She's very dedicated."

For another ten minutes, Gina told the entire story. Having been trumped in some ways, Mrs. Spark listened politely, not one barb. And once Gina had proceeded down the path of deceiving her older neighbor, there was no way to turn around. Their relationship was built on these foundations, topics from the first afternoon: Mrs. Spark's negligent son, Gina's good daughter, and there was no changing the routine once it had begun.

14

When Gina went over the events in her mind, it seemed like a dream yet here she was, sitting on an airplane to Korea. A woman had taken the middle seat. Young and thin, wearing dark jeans and a black blazer over a striped shirt. A thick gold bracelet on her right wrist, a sparkling wedding ring on her left hand. She unclipped a leather briefcase and pulled a sheaf of papers out. From what Gina could tell, mostly numbers and charts.

She closed her eyes again. Around her, quiet voices and crinkling paper. Soon, she felt the slow movement of the plane. She thought about watching the take-off but remembered she was over the wing. She was very tired. Images came and went: Mrs. Spark wielding the telephone and smiling up at Paul on the porch, Nehra dabbing at the small gash on Gina's knee, Deborah's shoulders shaking as she cried at their dad's funeral, her hair falling out of place for once. Teenaged Ian lying on his bed, the encyclopedia opened in front of him, crumbs in an unnatural shade of orange outlining his lips. The pretty teacher in *Dangerous Minds*, reading the poem about death and talking about choice. The high-speed dance around the hall in *The King and I*, the endless gaze, the succession of children, one at a time, kissing Deborah Kerr's hand as it extended from her pale blue frock.

As the plane lifted into the air, Gina's stomach dropped, and her eyes blinked open. She had smudged her glasses, so she wiped the lenses on the front of her sweater and put them back on.

A few months after her father died, she had interviewed for the job at Mr. Seutter's office. Her friend, Linda, had taken a job in the accounting department; her husband knew someone through his contacts at the stock exchange. She called to tell Gina about the opening for a secretary and although Gina was content with her job at Steadfast, the pay was better, and she'd recently been thinking about getting her own apartment.

Things at home were the same as ever, for the most part. Ian and her mother had cleared out the family room, deciding which books and magazines to keep and which to take to the Salvation Army. Many of them were piled in a corner of Ian's room and although Helen was a proponent of orderliness and Things Having Their Place, she allowed him this indulgence.

Helen went about her usual business, the cooking and cleaning and occasional chats with a few friends. Mrs. McDermott increased her neighborly efforts, stopping by at least weekly with baked goods or a few women's magazines. Gina grew to appreciate her efforts, the way she committed to being there and followed through. It seemed like a big thing, showing up. Sometimes Gina would walk into the kitchen and see the two women sitting across from each other at the table, holding coffee mugs or wine glasses depending on the time of day, chatting or staring at some vantage point beyond the gondola-covered curtains, lost in thought.

Partly because of the attention from Mrs. McDermott and partly because Ian seemed to be keeping up his menagerie of friends and interests, Gina felt justified striking out on her own. She got the job with Mr. Seutter, rented her first apartment, and continued her social activities—drinks with friends, movies, Wednesday dinners with the family. If her mother had an appointment or something to do in the city, she'd drop Ian at Gina's apartment, where he loved to lounge on the couch and talk. They'd walk down to the drugstore for scoops of ice cream, like they had as kids, or rent movies to watch on her VCR. He wasn't embarrassed to be seen with her, even at fourteen, at fifteen, at sixteen.

The flight attendant pushed a cumbersome tray down the aisle. The man took water and the young woman in the middle seat asked for 7-Up.

"A screwdriver, please," Gina said, as casually as she could. Nobody seemed to care. She arranged the napkin on her tray, the plastic cup on top.

Over their heads, the seatbelt light was turned off. The woman next to her reclined the seat slightly and crossed one ankle over her leg. She wore black boots with three-inch heels. Gina couldn't understand how she could travel in them. Sipping her drink, Gina pulled up the shade of her window, which afforded an eyeful of riveted steel and a row of slats fluttering in the wind. At the top of the oval window: a thin strip of blue.

"Excuse me, but could I have some vodka to mix with this?"

The flight attendant stood at the end of the row, again with the cart, and the well-dressed woman to Gina's left had stopped her. She looked at Gina and shrugged. "Changed my mind," she said.

Gina watched as the woman unscrewed the mini bottle of vodka—Stolichnaya brand—and poured a finger-width into the plastic glass, shimmering now with cubes of ices. She lifted the drink. "Cheers."

They touched glasses, careful not to spill. The woman was quite young, Gina could see that now, and she had a smattering of freckles across the bridge of her nose and hair the color of carrot cake.

"My stomach's a little upset," the woman said. "Maybe this will calm it."

Gina nodded.

"I'm LaRae," she said.

"Gina. Nice to meet you."

The woman took a long drink of the vodka and 7-Up, the ice cubes crowding against her upper lip. "It's such a long flight," she said. "I always think, I'll have the dinner, watch the movie, sleep. But I never do. Sleep, I mean. Then I spend the first day all haggard, in and out of offices where it's hard enough to keep track of what's being said." She refreshed her drink with more of the Stolichnaya.

"You travel for your job?" Gina asked.

She nodded. "I work for a financial company. One of my big clients is in Japan. I fly to Tokyo once a month, usually spend about five days."

Gina watched as she scratched her left wrist, at a spot that was already red and flaky. "That sounds exciting."

"Does it?"

"This is my first time out of the United States."

The woman's eyes widened. "Really? Why Tokyo?"

"I need to see my brother in Korea," she said. "I'm sorry, what was your name again?"

"LaRae."

Gina set down her drink, almost finished. "What a nice name. Is that Spanish?"

LaRae sputtered 7-Up and vodka, back into the wide-mouthed cup. "Sorry, no. I haven't heard that before."

"The way it sounds—"

She touched Gina's arm, warm pressure over the white sweater. "No, you're right. Gina, right?"

"Yes."

"My mother made it up. She's black and yes, I know I don't look it. As it turns out, I favor my father's Tennessee side, almost completely. Funny thing, genetics."

"Oh."

"Usually, people have to let that soak in for a minute."

Gina looked at her again. Green eyes, the freckles, pale skin. But now she noticed the young woman's hair. "Do you like traveling? For your job, I mean?"

LaRae fluttered her wrist, the gold bracelet resettling further down her arm. "I don't mind it, most of the time."

"It must be hard to leave your family."

"I'm engaged but not married yet. No kids. But yeah, it's hard to go sometimes. Do you have family in Chicago?"

"A brother," Gina said. "I have a sister in California."

"You're not married?"

She shook her head.

LaRae touched her arm again. "Sorry to be nosy." She leaned her head against the seat cushion.

"It's fine."

"A long day, about to get longer."

Gina saw moisture bubbling between LaRae's fluttering eyelashes. "Are you all right?"

As LaRae reached down into her briefcase, a tear escaped. She pulled out a packet of tissues. "My wedding is planned for June," she said. "But I'm having, as they say, doubts."

For some reason, Gina thought of the broker from long ago. If she were to open a dictionary to the word "doubt," she'd fully expect to see a picture of him. His doubts, her doubts. It seemed the perfect word to describe what had taken place between them.

LaRae patted the corners of her eyes with a tissue, careful to salvage her mascara. She pivoted in her seat. "This is going to sound very vague," she said. "But I'm not sure he loves me the way he's supposed to."

Gina nodded an encouragement.

"It seems to me, you shouldn't want to change someone, at least not at first. I'm aware I sound like a self-help book and maybe that's where all this is coming from, you know, our modern tendencies. We're entirely too educated. Our grandparents didn't sit around wondering about unconditional love. They did their job and made a garden where they could."

"I'm sure it'll work out," Gina said.

"It always does, right?" She raised her drink to clink against Gina's but noticed hers was empty.

As if on cue, the flight attendant breezed by, throwing brief, non-committal glances from side to side.

"Ma'am?" LaRae called.

The tall woman with tired eyes turned around and waited.

LaRae smiled, holding up her cup. "Could I bother you for another bottle of vodka, please, and another can of 7-Up?"

The woman's eyebrows arched under the shiny sweep of her bangs. "It'll be another charge," she said, not kindly.

"Oh, that's fine," LaRae answered, ignoring the woman's tone and almost making it seem the flight attendant was apologizing for having to charge for the drink.

Gina would have been mortified to be called out like that in public. But there was something about young women, the professional types. Something had hardened them, made them unafraid. They navigated through stores, through transactions, through business trips, completely entitled. It was exactly the way she imagined Amanda Blevin would have handled the encounter. Her sister Deborah could slice people in two with determined kindness.

When the beverages came, LaRae split both the vodka and the 7-Up between their two cups. They didn't talk anymore about the fiancé or Gina's brother but sat for a time in comfortable silence.

Gina paged through the airline magazine, her eyes not really settling on anything until she found the map of the Tokyo airport at the back. Terminal one, where United flights disembarked, was outlined in blue and shaded in gray. The shape of the building was foreign, not unlike a symbol from their strange language, with one long arm jutting to the left and two shorter branches extending down like legs. There were oval areas in two corners, like buds sprouting from the open, central space, and around these and down the long arm and one of the legs, a series of numbers denoting the terminal's gates. It didn't seem like a building at all; didn't seem like any sort of map she'd ever seen, and slight thump made its way to her heart.

"The airport's got a violent history," LaRae said, noticing the map.

Gina looked up, mired in thoughts of getting lost, of disappointing Ian and forgetting, for a split second, where she was.

"Protesters attacked police when it opened. In fact, the opening was delayed because someone drove a burning car into the control tower and destroyed it.

They were socialists," she said. "They thought the airport was being built for the U.S. military. For capitalism, basically."

"When was this?" Gina asked, thinking they were flying into some conflict, on top of having to find her way to the next flight.

LaRae drained her second drink. "In the seventies."

Gina closed the magazine and stuffed it into the narrow canvas flap where it belonged. Overhead, several small screens descended from the ceiling and blinked to life.

"I guess we missed the headsets," LaRae said. "Do you want one? I'll go ask."

"No, thanks," Gina said. "I'm very tired. I'll try to sleep for a while." Normally, she would have liked the diversion of a movie, but she had to keep her wits about her, had to stay focused on what she was doing. *This is everything to us*, Ian had said. He'd never been embarrassed by her that she was aware of, and she didn't want to give him a reason now.

Gina looked up as they showed a preview of the featured movie, one she hadn't seen. The edges of the screen were blurred, the subject in the center, a man, in full and bright focus. He stood stiffly, waving and speaking, a broad smile spreading across his face. He almost seemed fake, in that orchestrated moment, with the brilliant colors and intense scrutiny. *The Truman Show*, it was called. She'd have to rent it some other time when everything was settled.

She took off her glasses and found the brown case for them in her purse. The movie screens were entirely blurred now, flashing light and blobs of color, the sounds gurgling from many headsets around her: tiny, muted, and unfathomable. She folded her coat into a square, pressed it against the side of the airplane and leaned her head on top. Determined to rest, she forced her jittery eyelids closed.

15
Berwyn, May 1996.

Helen, propped up by pillows, adjusted the collar of a flowered nightgown. "Tell me the truth, Regina May."

Gina flinched. Her full name was invoked rarely and almost never in a positive way. "They want warm weather, Mom."

Helen puckered. "There's no guarantee of warm weather in June. Do you remember your friend, what was her name?"

Gina sat on one of the two dining room chairs that had been placed in her mother's bedroom for visitors. "Yes, but that was in April. You can't plan an outdoor wedding in April."

"April, June." Helen collapsed into the pillows. "I know why they changed the date."

"They're anxious," Gina said. "And maybe the hall was booked for September." The "maybe" covered the fact that she was making it up.

Deborah entered with a tray and a caricatured smile. "Hot tea and biscuits."

Helen perked up. "Who made biscuits?"

"They're cookies," Gina said.

"If we're having an afternoon tea, English-style, we might as well have biscuits." Deborah placed the tray next to Helen on the bed and sat beside it. "In honor of our great-great-great grandpa on Dad's side."

"We were talking about the wedding," Helen looked at Deborah. "What do you think of her?"

Pretending to weigh her answer, Deborah stirred sugar into her mother's tea. "She's wonderful. Just what Ian needs."

"How do you know what he needs?" Gina asked.

"Everybody needs—" She bit her lower lip. "I guess I don't. But he seems happy."

Helen nodded. "That's what I thought."

Gina watched their mother sip the tea, her liver-marked hands and sharp elbows, the ever-present lines radiating from her mouth. At times like this, when she was doing something mundane, when she set the mug down and her first finger stayed looped around the handle in such a *normal* way, it was hard to believe her body was being erased from the inside. At other times, such as evening, such as an hour or so before her dosage, when her knuckles turned white against the sheets and her forehead glistened, when she barked at Ian for talking too loudly, for laughing too much, for bringing the wrong crossword puzzle book—at these times her cancer crowded them with its enormity.

"My ride will be here soon." Deborah said. "Can you think of anything else you need, Mom?"

Gina traced the seam of her trousers with her finger. "I could drive you to the airport."

Deborah looked over, her eyes surprisingly red. "That's all right. Cheryl doesn't mind. I haven't had a chance to talk to her much this trip."

Gina wanted to say: It's not a *trip*, not like the vacations you've taken with your old high school friends, with Cheryl and Susan and Johanna. A spa weekend in Sedona or that week, an entire week in Maui, where I've never been. It's not one of your regular, infrequent visits home, Deborah, when you stay at Cheryl's house because she has so much more room than I do, and you meet us at restaurants and tell us all your plans for the *hometown* part of your trip, before you head downtown for shows I haven't seen. She said, instead, "Okay."

Deborah's hair was still blonde, flipped up in the back and curled under around her face. All in all, it looked like something that took an hour to arrange. Even for this, a day of sitting around with her sick mother, she had made time for mascara and perfume. Gina respected it, envied it, and despised it all at once.

Deborah looked up, as if remembering something. "Sorry I never made it to your condo this time, Gina. How long have you had it now?"

"Almost a year," she answered. "My first place."

"But you had that little apartment," Helen said.

"And the brownstone, for years," Deborah added.

"The first place I've owned."

Both nodded, understanding the distinction.

"There's always next time," Gina said.

A vibration hovered in the room. The three women sat, all slightly uncomfortable. Deborah in her guilt for leaving and Helen in her fear and discomfort and more guilt; to Gina, it felt like some wonderful bond between her sister and mother in which she had no part. And it made her angry, always being a third wheel with them and the understanding and wordless complicity they had and having no outlet or cause, she looked around, struggling. "Where did you find that old quilt, anyway?" she said.

Helen, eyebrows raised, looked down at Grandma Sahlin's quilt and clutched it defensively.

Gina knew she had scored a direct hit. But the remorse came quickly because really, she loved the quilt and would want it draped on her own sick bed, should the time come.

"It's Grandma's," Deborah said, needlessly.

Gina rose. "I'm going to have some tea, too. Should I take the tray?"

Helen, back to herself, eyes narrowed. "I'm not finished."

"Okay."

In the kitchen, Ian sat at the table, reading the newspaper. He looked up when Gina entered. "What's wrong?"

She shook her head, sat next to him on the remaining chair. "Do you remember when Daddy died?"

Ian crossed his hands over the paper, oddly enough, in an exact copy of a gesture their father used to make.

"You were, what, thirteen?" she asked.

"Yes."

"You probably don't remember some things."

"Like what?"

She shrugged. "I don't know. The service. The way we all had to wait outside the funeral home because there was a mix-up, and they weren't ready for us when we arrived. The way Mom never cried."

"Wait a minute," Ian said. "Mom cried."

"I never saw it," Gina said, close to tears herself. "I never did."

Ian stood up and motioned her over to the back door, near the window. The blue gondolas on the curtains were faded; dark stains ran vertically in the creases of the fabric.

"I don't know what you're saying." He ran fingers through his dark curls, which he had cut shorter since meeting Carrie. "She had three children and I think in a situation like that, you postpone your own grieving."

She looked up, wishing to put her head on his shoulder. "Postpone?"

"You know, delay until later."

"I know what postpone means!"

"Okay, okay." He walked to the sink and filled a glass with water.

"How many glasses have you had today?" Ian was trying a new diet, one that involved drinking huge amounts of water.

"This is my ninth," he said.

"Three more to go?"

He smiled. "Yep. I'm trying to get down to a size forty-six tuxedo."

"I'm glad you moved up the wedding," Gina said. "It'll be great to have Mom there, while she's still—"

"I know." He finished his water and moved closer. "Listen, we've got to hold it together, you and me."

She nodded.

"When it comes down to it, I'm not sure about Deborah, how much help she'll be," he said. "But Gina, you know Mom loves you."

She started to turn away, but he grabbed her arm. "She had to be strong when Daddy died. She's got limitations. We all do. But she loves you."

"How do you know?" Gina felt silly for asking and though aware of the melodrama—even as it was happening—she couldn't stop herself.

He patted her arm, let his hand drop. "Because she's your mother. You should give her a break sometimes. You're not the most affectionate person yourself."

Her jaw dropped. How could he, of all people, think she wasn't affectionate? He used to burrow into her lap for Saturday morning cartoons, grab her hand whenever they walked to the park.

Their family home was on Euclid Street, a street like the ones surrounding it, one block from the busier Oak Park Avenue and a ten-minute stroll from the tangled shade trees of Proksa Park. Gina could see and feel it still: Ian's clammy hand in hers as they counted cracks in the sidewalk, two peanut butter sandwiches wrapped in wax paper, the grass tickling their necks as they stared up through angled branches at pockets of blue sky. The house itself, red brick and white shutters, a heavy door that squeaked welcomes and goodbyes, the smell of cooking and baking, of sweat on the humid days that drove them to the front room and its large, swiveling fan. After their father died, Gina moved out for the first time but returned to help with Ian, then moved out a second time to the brownstone, for good.

"Which do you think is a better wedding song," Ian asked, "*You Were Meant for Me* or *Who Will Save Your Soul?*"

"What?" Gina shook herself back to present.

Ian sat down again. "You know the singer, Jewel?" He sang in a horrible falsetto, "You were meant for me, and I was meant for you."

"Sounds familiar," she said, without conviction.

"We both like her, but Carrie likes another song, and I don't really think it's a love song at all."

"How would I know?"

Ian frowned. "What do you *think*? The name of it is *Who Will Save Your Soul?* Does that sound like a song you play at a wedding?"

She leaned against the counter. "Maybe Carrie thinks she's saving your soul. But then, I'm not very good with these emotional things, as you've pointed out."

He looked at the ceiling with the patient exasperation of a man who has spent his life surrounded by women. Then, he grinned. "Personally, I think we should all get our groove on to *Macarena*."

"Oh, no," she said. "If I hear that song one more time—"

And before she could stop him, Ian rose and began to sing in another version of his horrible singing voice, with a bit more tenor, and he performed the hand motions associated with the song.

"*When I dance, they call me Macarena, and the boys they say that I'm buena—*"

"How do you even know the words?" Gina asked, covering her face with her hands.

"*They all want me; they can't have me. Ahhhh, Macarena!*"

"Ian!" she warned, looking towards the bedroom.

But it was too late. He was warming up. He bent his knees and put his hands behind his head, then on his hips, and the sight was too funny, with his sloppy button-down shirt and baggy jeans, his short curly hair all askew.

"*Na, na, la, la cuca Macarena. La vata shimmy Macarena.*"

"That's not right," she said, laughing. A few more lines of the convoluted chorus, the Spanish portions he had no idea how to sing, and she turned to leave the kitchen.

At that moment, Deborah appeared at the door, supporting their mother by the elbow. Helen, flowered nightgown hanging over her frame, all sharp edges and pallid skin, the amused expression on her face somehow making it even worse, this image, this vestige of the vital person she used to be; that moment, when the world stopped moving and Gina felt as though her whole body was in a drawn out gasp, at the vision of her mother standing at the entrance to her beloved kitchen, wanting to hear what was going on, needing perhaps a moment of the old times, drawn to the well of Ian's exuberance as they all sometimes were, and Gina could think only in fragments and pangs. Her mother's arm reaching across her torso, clicking the seatbelt into the chrome receptacle, years before seatbelts were regularly used by everyone else. One sticky, summer day, her mother bolting out of the house to chase down the boy who'd bloodied Ian's lip, standing on the lawn in a fury, looking up and down the street for release. The pinch of her mother's grip, in the soft flesh on the underside of her arm, when she was misbehaving. Her mother, at the house after a day of school, a day of play, usually sitting at her kitchen table with a magazine or something to crochet, or sometimes with nothing at all. Her mother, a constant. Seeing her gaunt arms, remembering the warm strength of them as they crossed over, bracing her, to see the same arms now, hanging lifelessly from the folds of the nightgown—

Even then, Gina didn't realize the full impact.

Three weeks later, Deborah was back from California because there was a sudden decline. The hospice nurse assured them this was often the case, this quick plummet, and when Helen stopped eating, they were advised the end would come soon. Gina took a leave of absence from work and Ian came each day after finishing his sales route at the paper company. The days at the house were long and eerily quiet. Gina and Deborah watched hours of television, reruns and soap operas, whatever was on. When they needed groceries or supplies, Gina would go. She had her used Honda Accord then, which, like their mother, had seen healthier days. By the time Ian came in the evenings, they were starved for the break.

After eight days of round-the-clock vigilance, their mother was gone. One day they were still waiting and the next, it was over. Even though it was expected, it felt like an ambush. Gina was mostly unprepared. Not like the immediate shock of her father's death; no, a completely different loss.

And Ian had been wrong about Deborah, for it was their older sister who came through in the end with the unpleasant, unspeakable tasks, with the nuts and bolts of what needed to be done. She rose to the occasion, bathing their mother, changing her bandages, diapers, and nightgowns and afterwards, making funeral arrangements and plans for the house, calling all of Helen's friends and scattered family.

Ian and Carrie moved the wedding, which Helen had missed after all, back to September. The hall for the reception had plenty of availability then.

16

A flock of white and gray gulls plummets from the sky, skimming in a mass of extended wings over the water. Their pink, short legs are pulled up against bright feathers; yellowish eyes are alert. On a long and narrow dock, they line up and look out over the inlet. Feathers ruffled, heads withdrawn against the cold wind, storing up their strength for another tour of Tokyo Bay. The gusts are strong on this sunny afternoon and the gulls should be able to ride the currents to considerable elevation, conserving their powerful flaps for when they're needed, making the flight efficient and effective. They have no way of knowing, queued on that man-made extension and overlooking the archipelago of other man-made forms, that soon, during the anticipated flight, two of their own will become separated in a particularly vicious swell of air, and these same two birds will remain together in the sky, not understanding how they diverged from the others, straining to get their bearings and then, sensing the flock some distance away, will increase their efforts to rejoin it, one bird flying quite higher than the other, having been picked up by one of the currents they hope for in better times, both birds single-mindedly pushing towards the far-off mass of gray figures dotting the blue expanse, the lower bird instinctively pushing forward but also beginning to rise, wanting to accompany the other one but suddenly prevented by the rotating blades of a United 747, inbound from the United States.

For the moment, however, the birds huddle and wait. The wind whistles through the buildings of Tokyo, over the smooth runways accented with paint, makes the water of the bay turbulent. And the gulls wait for some message from the earth, some vibration understood in unison, at which point they will stand on their pink, dappled legs and rise.

Gina's head rolled to the right, the tendon in her neck stretching painfully. She opened her eyes to the navy fabric of the seat cushion, which protruded on each side to prevent heads rolling around as hers had. Her eyes were gritty, her throat dry. She looked at her watch. One hour until they were supposed to reach Tokyo. Two hours for her layover, then another two hours on the flight to Seoul. Closer and closer.

She retrieved her coat from where it had slipped down next to the wall of the plane. Unfolding it, she draped it over her legs. She had a post-sleep chill; her entire body, it seemed, was covered in gooseflesh. From her lap she opened the brown leather case that held her glasses and put them on.

LaRae turned and smiled. "Almost over," she said, pointing to the closest movie screen, about four rows ahead of them. The black wires of United's complimentary earphones dangled next to her copper hair. "They kept having to start it over for some reason."

Gina pulled her shoulders back in a stretch.

The flight attendant came by, collecting trash. She took her time with this, much more time than she had with the second call for drinks. Gina wondered if the crew had to stay on the airplane afterwards, picking up crumpled food wrappers and plastic cups crushed in the magazine holder. She looked tired, this woman, her blonde hair still styled but some sections starting to unravel, her eyes red-rimmed and her makeup a faded version of what it once was. "Trash?" she asked, offering the open mouth of a black garbage bag.

Gina shook her head and in a surge of clarity, thought, "Enough." Her coat and purse were shoved under the seat in front of her. She turned her legs to the side, her sweater catching for a moment under the armrest shared with LaRae. She grabbed the leather strap of her purse, gave it a tug and once in her lap, unzipped it. She moved aside her wallet and a hairbrush and shimmied from the bottom a manila envelope, folded in half. She bent the metal tongs and opened the flap. Peeking inside, she could read the header on the first sheet: Dr. Raymond Trainor, M.D., and his address, the same one in Berwyn where she had seen him so many years before. Of course, it had been some time since Dr. Trainor had passed away. The records had been in storage until the ambitious Sandra Pierce, R.N., who now worked at an entirely different office, had decided to see what she could do about disbursing them.

For a long time, Gina had avoided doctors. It wasn't a conscious decision. They were busy years, with many changes and much to keep her occupied. Shortly after her father died, she rented her first apartment. She had recently started the job at Mr. Seutter's office, but she still went for an occasional dinner with Bonnie and Linda, or with Sandy, a secretary she'd met at the new office. On the weekends, she shopped for clothes or things for the apartment. She remembered buying a set of potholders, bright yellow and covered in sunbursts. They were so cheerful she kept them on the counter instead of buried in a drawer. Other items held special meaning: a set of drinking glasses, much more delicate than the thick marbled ones her mother always used, a dining set with mauve-colored, upholstered chairs. On Wednesdays, she had dinner at her childhood home. Ian would finish his homework before Gina arrived from the train and walked over. At first, she'd bring something for the three of them to eat but in time, Helen started cooking again, setting the table with some festivity, wearing her fancy blouse.

As for her own health, Gina gave it little thought. She understood the admonition Dr. Trainor had given her and figured as long as she steered clear of a similar situation, she'd be fine. From time to time, she did notice a slight surge where her heart was concerned, but she took care not to get herself in trouble again.

Unbelievable how quickly years could pass. It must have been 1988 or 1989 before she started seeing Doctor Tam, down the street from her office. She'd been having a tooth ache, one of her molars. She found the benefits package she'd been given at the start of the year, looked up a nearby dentist in the booklet, and made an appointment. One day on her lunch hour, she walked over.

The dentist was a short, fat, humorless man who scolded her for avoiding cleanings and exams. A woman came in to scrape the plaque from Gina's teeth, then the dentist returned and found two cavities in addition to the ailing tooth, which needed a root canal. On one of the several forms she had to fill out when she entered the office, there was a list of conditions. "Now or in the past, have you had," and a long line of boxes to check Yes or No:

Birth defects or hereditary problems?

Bone fractures or major injuries?

Diabetes or low sugar?

Kidney problems?

Cancer, tumor, radiation, or chemotherapy?

Sexually transmitted diseases?

Hepatitis, jaundice, or other liver problems?

Mental health disturbance, or depression?

High or low blood pressure?

Excessive bleeding, bruising, or anemia?

Heart defects, heart murmur, rheumatic heart disease?

Angina, arteriosclerosis, stroke, or heart attack?

Frequent headaches or migraines?

A variety of emotions surfaced as she read the list. Mostly, fear that after a decade of avoidance, she may have some of the conditions, and guilt for being irresponsible for so long. She was in her thirties then, living in the brownstone near her mother's home. A regular grown-up. Even Ian was grown, graduated from college, and working at Parchment Inc. She needed to set a better example.

But the main thing, the action that started everything else that would come, was when she took the pencil and put a tiny checkmark in one Yes box, for the heart murmur that Dr. Trainor had detected many years before.

She had no way of knowing that dental patients who have a heart murmur often need to have antibiotics before certain procedures. She couldn't have predicted the dentist would be unwilling to move forward with the root canal until Gina had obtained clearance from her primary physician (which, technically, she didn't have).

Her lower jaw throbbing, she returned to the office and looked up the closest primary care physician. Dr. Tam, at 42 Washington. Another appointment later that day, the confirmation of the heart murmur, two phone calls and the faxing of documents, and three days later, Gina had her root canal after lunch and took an early train home.

"Yes, I hear it." Dr. Tam had leaned over, her straight hair tucked behind each ear, pressing the stethoscope she had warmed between her palms to Gina's chest. "It's minor," she had said. "Nothing to worry about."

Gina didn't want to explain. Dr. Tam wasn't aware of Gina's history, didn't know what had happened and really, had taken only a cursory look. Get the tooth fixed, that's what mattered.

But in the spirit of adult responsibility Gina had aspired to when thinking of Ian, she started having regular check-ups. Blood pressure, cholesterol, pap smears. This last thing was entirely unpleasant but after several, she learned to relax. A necessity, something to grit your teeth through. At her first appointment with Dr. Tam, she filled out more forms. One asked for information about her previous doctor and Gina told the receptionist she couldn't remember the name or address. They asked a few more times, and she always said that she'd look at home and call with the details. Eventually, they stopped asking.

Yes, she'd been fortunate to avoid any serious health problems and here she was, forty-five years old.

Besides the few dates orchestrated by Nehra, there had been one other relationship, in 1983. A nice man she met at a fundraiser, one of Mr. Seutter's events. They had dinners, saw movies, but it had burned out quickly. Donald Graham. Probably married now, with three kids and a loud, active house.

Gina glanced at the sliver of blue over the metal wing of the plane, then pulled the small sheaf of papers from the envelope. She was surprised to see how far back the records went. Immunizations, weight checks. Prescription of iron supplement at two years of age. The referral for corrective lenses. The time she fell off her bicycle and had three stitches at the side of her elbow, so that every time she extended her arm, they stretched and pulled, and she was afraid she'd tear them. "You must be careful!" the old women at the park had yelled when they pulled her up with their thin, shaky arms.

Gina flipped through the pages, found the entry for January 12, 1977. The papers were divided into sections: the original sheets from the file, secured through two holes with metal tongs like the ones on the envelope, and underneath, another set of pages, typed up by Dr. Trainor's staff as a summary of the notes. His original handwriting was almost completely illegible. Certain words jumped out from his handwritten entry that day; she remembered him scrawling as she waited on the high table. He must have filled in more after she left, because the page for that day was half full.

No indication... young female... arrhythmia detected... distraught... twenty-three years ... pelvic... no sign.

Gina rifled through until she found the typed version of the doctor's notes for the same day. She read it slowly.

"A young female patient, twenty-three years of age. Date of last exam, four years prior. No indication of mental disturbance (concern relayed). Patient seemed distraught, preoccupied. Slight arrhythmia detected. Innocent murmur. Patient worried about late menstrual cycle and possible pregnancy. Performed pelvic exam. No sign present. All appeared normal. Spoke to patient about effect of stress on cycle."

The typed version ended with the following, dated a week later, "Follow-up call with father of patient. Nothing further."

Gina slid the papers into the envelope, folded the whole thing and pushed it back into her purse. Outside her window, clouds drifted by in hazy sheets, cut and separated by the jutting wingspan of the aircraft. Beyond the steel promontory, the sky behind the blurring of clouds was serious blue, a kind of blue you couldn't see from the ground. Gina wished suddenly, fervently, that her view to land wasn't blocked, so deserted she felt, so rootless.

The seatbelt sign illuminated and chimed. Over the PA system, the flight attendant announced in a canned voice they would soon begin the descent. All tray tables must be returned to the upright position, all carry-on items returned to the space under the seat.

Next to her, LaRae sniffled and brought a crumpled tissue to her face. Gina followed the direction of LaRae's gaze to the movie screen. Across a vivid plane of blue, a lone sailboat drifted. There'd been a storm. Everything was wind-blown and wet. The man from the beginning of the movie was on the boat, a thick-cabled sweater belted into his pants. Something had knocked him down, but he strained to get up. The rope for the sail was next to him; he grabbed it and began to pull. Slowly, the sail rose, and the scene cut to a bird's eye shot of the boat, righted, slicing through the accommodating water. For a few inspiring moments, he was happy, triumphant. Sun on his face, wind lifting his hair.

LaRae noticed Gina was watching. She pulled one earphone out. "Crying like a baby," she said, shaking her head.

"What happened?"

"His life was a television show. Nothing was real."

They looked back at the screen.

The boat jerked to a stop because its bow had pierced the edge of the sky. The man was thrown forward. Again, he got up. He crawled to the front of the boat and placed his hand against the sky, which was really a thin wall painted to look like the sky.

"What do you mean?" Gina whispered.

"It's not reality. Everything was a lie." LaRae held up her hand when she said the last part, because a man in a beige beanie began to speak to the man on the boat and she wanted to listen. The new man, shown from a cold room, seemed to have some sort of control over the whole situation. Right away Gina rooted for the man sailing. He had such a defeated air, his shoulders slumping under the heavy sweater, his eyes having lost the zeal from the start of the movie.

No indication of mental disturbance (concern relayed).

What did that have to do with anything, her mental state? Dr. Trainor was a general practitioner. He measured her growth when she was a child, gave her immunizations. What did that mean, "concern relayed?" Who relayed a concern? "Mental disturbance?"

There was only one person who had spoken to Dr. Trainor besides her.

Gina strained her mind, remembering things at the house during that time. She worked, she met the broker at Benny's sometimes, she helped her mother around the house. She and her father had the usual interactions. They talked about work at the dinner table. Why would he have questioned her mental state? Why ask Dr. Trainor? And why did Dr. Trainor lie on his report? Why had he written nothing about the baby?

Suddenly, the right side of the airplane dipped. Several rows behind Gina, a loud gasp was followed by a high voice.

"Oh my God, oh my God."

Many people still had earphones on for the movie, but those who didn't twisted in their seats, craning their necks.

"Fire. It's fire. Oh my God."

Flight attendants converged from the front and the back of the plane. One of them, a skinny woman with glasses, rushed to the passenger who was yelling. Muffled voices, then quick footsteps as two more flight attendants rushed by.

"What's happening?" A man stood in the aisle. Red-faced, well-dressed, expensive watch. Someone accustomed to having his questions answered.

"One moment, Sir."

The flight attendants scurried about, positioned themselves at the front, middle and back of the plane in some sort of preconceived configuration.

Across the row, on the other side, someone unbelted their seatbelt and went to talk to the woman who'd announced, "Fire." They all watched this woman, their new representative, to see what she'd uncover.

The flight attendant in the back, the blonde, grabbed the representative's arm and spoke in her ear.

Gina's heart thumped like an anvil against her chest wall. She turned around. On the movie screen, the man stood in front of a door that had opened in the wall of the blue sky. The dark rectangle framed him, all darkness, offering no glimpse of what lay beyond.

There was no daughter, Gina imagined herself saying to Mrs. Spark. I created her, made her up. She could picture the look of disbelief on the old woman's face, the way she'd crunch up her features then let them expand again. Gina would say: I liked to think about what it would've been like, if things had been different, if the baby had made it. She was sure to gain some sympathy from Mrs. Spark if she told her about the day at Dr. Trainor's. About what came afterwards. She'd start by bringing the old woman a gift, something from Korea. They'd sit for tea, as they had many times before. She'd explain that if she'd had a daughter, she'd have more in common with Mrs. Spark. Something to talk about. She'd tell her about the notebooks, the letters she wrote and how they always made her feel better. That sometimes she woke in a muddled state before the world materialized and believed she did have a daughter, whose name was Michelle and who taught disadvantaged high school kids in California. She'd ask Mrs. Spark if she remembered what it was like to be a child, your parents invulnerable, your life full of dreams. She'd say having Michelle was like that, like being young again, and she wasn't sure she could give up the feeling, the possibility of what could have been.

"Attention, Ladies and Gentlemen." The PA system crackled to life.

The movie paused, the man suspended in the dark doorway, sky and clouds surrounding him.

"This is your captain speaking. We've had a minor incident this afternoon."

The airplane lurched a bit, a slight pulling and pushing. Isolated sounds of panic echoed throughout the cabin.

"Please remain calm," he said. "We've had a bird strike on the right side of the airplane. We've lost power in that engine."

Murmurs echoed around the cabin and from one corner, a stifled sob.

Gina pressed her hands over her chest, trying to calm her heart, which thudded steadily, hotly, an autonomous force. She had always thought it would be her heart. It didn't seem fair that someone who hardly ever flew, someone who took so many precautions— Her thoughts were a jumble. Will we drown? If I can't see Ian again— Her throat clenched.

"We're trained to fly an aircraft with one engine," the voice said. "There's no need to worry, only a few adjustments to be made. We've got about a hundred more miles to New Tokyo International, and we anticipate a safe landing."

What else would they say? Gina thought. No one can prepare you, warn you against such a thing. Chilled again, she brought her coat up and over her shoulders. She'd been carrying it all day and finally, it had come in handy.

"Please keep your seats upright and your seatbelts buckled. We should have you on the ground shortly."

For the next fifteen minutes, the cabin was coated in silence. The flight attendants came back through with trash bags for one final sweep, exhibiting stubborn smiles. Or at least that's how it seemed to Gina, because most likely, they weren't telling the whole truth.

Clinging to the lapels of her coat, running over and over in her mind the events of that day, the visit to Dr. Trainor's, the silent car ride home, the loss, Gina stared at the sky still visible over the steel wingspan. The persistent hue seemed hopeful; the plane had stabilized and seemed to be, as the pilot had insisted, flying smoothly with one engine.

She remembered the cramping, the fear, the blood. It wasn't something you'd soon forget, like nothing that came before or after. And with a sense of certainty calming her violent heart, she straightened in her seat and waited. Two rows ahead, a woman rotated in her seat and looked back. Smooth, black hair cut bluntly like Carrie's, eyebrows like two lines of kohl. Gina closed her eyes.

17
Chicago, April 1997

The building was brick and tall, on the south side of the Loop, one of the industrial buildings recently reconceived as condominiums for young professionals. Gina didn't like the neighborhood because it was somewhat abandoned, with few conveniences nearby. Even the building itself was mostly empty, still under construction except for the one wing where Ian and Carrie had purchased their two-bedroom loft.

Gina pushed the button and waited for Carrie's voice on the intercom. In the crook of her arm, she had a Styrofoam container of chicken noodle soup from the restaurant in the lobby of her office building. The briny aroma drifted up and tugged at her stomach.

When Carrie stepped out of the elevator and over a roll of carpet left there, she looked disheveled and tired. Typically, she wore smart suits or fitted slacks and cardigans. Her hair was always smooth and shiny, and she usually wore the diamond earrings Gina knew for a fact had cost Ian a small fortune.

"I brought some soup," Gina told her. "Ian said you had a cold."

"Oh, yes," she said. "That's nice of you."

They stepped back onto the elevator, which didn't seem entirely trustworthy. The hardware hadn't been cleaned or updated ever; the buttons were surrounded in a gilded frame of gold, the lettering script from some other era.

"I hope you didn't have any problems getting here," Carrie said.

"Oh, no," she said. "I took a cab."

The elevator opened, and they followed the long hallway. Carrie opened a door and stepped aside, allowing Gina to pass. Inside, beams of wood crisscrossed the high ceiling, and industrial fixtures hung down on long cables. In the kitchen, a trio of red-shaded lights illuminated the marble counter. Gina set the bag there and started to take her coat off. It was spring in name only. Forty-one degrees when she left the office.

"Throw that over the couch." Carrie walked to a kitchen cupboard and stood on her toes to reach a set of wooden bowls. They sat on the stools, ladling soup with the wide spoons Carrie had provided. The utensil was so wide Gina had to stretch her mouth into an unnatural position to get the thing in.

"I almost forgot," Carrie said. "You want Chardonnay?"

Gina shrugged. "If you're having some."

She retrieved a coffee mug from behind the toaster and pulled down another one from the shelf. The Chardonnay came from a partially empty bottle, which she left on the counter after she poured.

"Ian's in Boston?" Gina asked.

"Yes. A regional meeting they have every year."

"I remember he's been there before."

Carrie nodded.

"How's your job?" Gina asked. "Does the doctor still do a lot of LASIK surgeries?"

"Tons." She took a big drink from the mug. "You should think about it."

"I should've done it earlier."

Carrie smiled. "Never too late." Suddenly, her eyes filled.

So much for avoiding the topic of the failed adoption. Gina patted Carrie's shoulder through the crumpled Michigan sweatshirt she wore.

They talked a bit more about Ian's trip, which hotel Parchment Inc. had reserved, where the meetings would take place and what he'd do on his free time. They talked about Carrie's family in Benton Harbor, one brother in dentistry school and the other currently unemployed. Carrie talked about the swampland of Michigan out of which her town had sprung and how as a kid, she had dreamed about getting away. Gina couldn't understand her feelings; from all indications, Carrie had enjoyed a typical, middle-class childhood. She'd met her parents at the wedding, and they seemed normal enough. This inclination in Carrie for wandering, the unsettled feeling Gina often sensed in her company, was the main, worrisome thing. If Carrie couldn't settle down, was never happy, what did that mean for Ian?

They finished their wine and Carrie reached across and pulled the bottle over. She poured refills. "I had a name picked out."

Gina considered taking off the buttoned sweater. She felt a bit flushed from the wine and thought of her heart. "He was a cute baby."

"Can you imagine," Carrie said, "someone taking your child away?"

Gina sipped her wine. "Did it help to take some time off?"

"I suppose. But I like working. That's something you should know about me. We agreed I would keep my job after the baby came."

"All right," she said.

Carrie blinked her shining, brown eyes. "You know, I never felt a true vocation like some people. I stumbled into my job, but I really love it."

"Ian says you might go back to school to become an optician?"

"Ophthalmologist," she said. "But that's a full medicine degree and I still have a semester to finish my Bachelor's. I always intended to go back."

"You will," Gina said.

"Ian says I should go for Optometry." She looked over. "They do eye exams, routine stuff."

"Is that less school?"

"Yes." She drank from the mug and set it down too loudly. "Oops." Rubbing her diamond-less earlobe, she stared at some point beyond the kitchen.

Gina knew she was thinking about the baby. She brought up Ian's trip again, but the room was full of Carrie's sorrow. "You and Ian have so much time," she said, finally. "It was so soon, I mean, after my mother."

Carrie's eyebrows tilted together. "What does that have to do with anything?"

She cleared her throat. "I think you'll have so many chances. If you relaxed about it—"

Carrie's eyes widened.

"—maybe you'd have your own babies."

"Oh, Gina, you have no idea what you're saying."

"You have everything. You're young and you've got Ian to do whatever you want. I'm sorry this happened to you, I am."

"But?"

Gina stood up, gathered the bowls and spoons, and took them to the sink. "But nothing. I'm sorry, that's all." She lifted the wine bottle, now empty. "Do you have any more of this?"

Carrie found another bottle and once again, reopened the wound of losing the blonde-haired baby. Listening was the least Gina could do, after saying what she'd said. Carrie rehashed the whole thing: the decision to adopt, filing of the papers, the first phone call, the blurry photo of the baby, the celebration and various purchases, the devastating news. When she had finished, Carrie sunk into a ball on the couch, where they had moved with the fresh bottle of wine.

"My mother chased a boy down the street once," Gina said.

Carrie looked up with bleary eyes. "What?"

"Ian was about eleven," she said. "Matthew Frame lived three streets over. We always knew him. Deborah babysat him and his older brother, Michael." She took a drink of wine and settled the mug on her belly. "One summer day, Matthew and Ian had a fight. Ian came home with a bloody lip. Our mother was furious. I'd never seen her like that. She ran out the front door and down the street. We stood on the porch watching her, and Ian said: 'She doesn't even know where she's going.'"

Carrie smiled.

"And sure enough, she ran to the end of the street, sort of paced around, then walked back to the house. Her hands were shaking while she drank a big glass of iced tea."

"Why are you telling me this story?"

Gina unbuttoned the first two buttons of her sweater. "You are stronger than you think, that's all. Because you can have—" she put her hand up to keep Carrie from protesting, "—or adopt other babies, but I can't. Deborah told me once having children was like losing pieces of your heart, one at a time. So maybe you've lost a little piece, but you still have your heart, you still have a chance." She stood up.

"What do you mean?" Carrie pulled her back to the couch. And without intending to, Gina told her story in fits and starts. The late period, the visit to Dr. Trainor's, her heart condition, the miscarriage that followed the doctor's exam. She was floating above the scene as she spoke, watching herself, appalled, relieved, knowing some divide had been crossed. Perhaps Carrie's grief was premature, even overdone, but it was still grief. The pain of losing a child. Gina had kept this story to herself for twenty years. Afterwards, silence settled. And then, Carrie started to ask questions. Gina got confused, walked through the cold loft, and barricaded herself in the bathroom.

Carrie's insistent voice came through the door, echoing in the cavernous space. "Don't you see, Gina? He couldn't have—he wouldn't have done that. Gina? Gina?" Eventually, she gave up.

In time, Gina dried her face and buttoned her cardigan. When the two women parted that evening, they said all the right things, thank-you-take-care-see-you-soon, and when Gina's low heels clunked onto the cement outside, there was only one direction to go. Steadily, she made her way towards home.

18

Another line for boarding, another settling in. Another flight, much shorter. From the outside, the airport in Korea was sprawling and unassuming. The plane taxied past a white tower with a bulb of glass on top, then alongside a long row of buildings. The main structure had a roof split into two u-shaped curves, like rain ducts set next to each other. This strange roof was Gina's first indication they had landed someplace new and different. The first building looked Oriental, with a sloped roof meeting at a point, flared edges. The next one, longer and shorter, was merely an endless row of windows with a green roof. Here and there, an enclosed extension jutted from between windows—tunnels for the passengers. The airplane meandered to a rectangle of concrete shaded more lightly than the rest and came to a stop.

Gina looked out the window at her narrow view. No wing obstruction for this brief, second flight. In the distance, cloud-coated mountains framed an area that seemed for the most part flat and unremarkable. The sky was hazy; everything green had turned to winter shades of gray and brown. The mountains were not terribly tall, but one was larger than the rest, flat on the top as though shorn. From the runway, asphalt paths branched to the left and right, dividing the open area into squares, most of which were outlined with the remaining snow from an earlier storm.

The plane from Tokyo to Seoul had been a smaller one, only two seats on each side of a narrow row. The second flight had lasted two hours if you counted the take-off and landing time, exactly as Ian had said. Gina gazed at the flat-topped mountain, solid and definite. It had been a long trip and now, to be so close.

Only a week had passed since Ian and Carrie had dropped the infant car seat on their way to the Babies R Us by Elmwood Park. They still needed a few things, they said; they didn't know for sure what size the baby would be and wanted to be prepared. Over time, Carrie and Gina had developed an uncomfortable comfort around each other. They were able to spend hours together, either at one of their homes or during the occasional Wednesday dinners, without ever really making eye contact. The comfortable part came from the reassurance that both knew the rules of engagement; the uncomfortable part was the memory of that night at the loft, the elephant in the room.

Gina stood and stretched her legs, anxious to get off the airplane. She waited for a young woman with a toddler in tow to pass, then it was her turn to enter the stream. The plane was parked some distance from the terminal. She blinked in the sunlight and followed the others to the metal steps attached to a white tunnel. Various figures stood at the glass of the airport windows. One could be Ian. She marveled for a moment at the distance she had travelled but didn't, even then, fully comprehend it.

Her eagerness mounted as she made her way to the end of the tunnel, where a square view of chairs, people and bright lights was visible. She stepped out and searched the room. Faces everywhere, a myriad of colors, a white ceiling accented with thousands of tiny vents, and finally, around a scuffed column, Ian.

"Meema," he said.

She stumbled the last few steps, overcome to see his kind face, his magnificent eyes, and she grabbed him around his mid-section, her purse falling awkwardly to her elbow and banging into his side.

His hand came to rest on her shoulder.

"You haven't lost any weight," she said into his sweater.

His chest rose with a few chuckles. "Since last weekend?"

She backed up and looked at him. "What about the Jenny Craig stuff?"

"I couldn't bring it with me, could I?" He looked at her purse and her coat, folded over one arm. "Do you have a scarf? Boots?"

"Packed," she told him, still holding on.

"Long flight?"

"It was fine. No problem."

He squirmed a little and she let go. She couldn't stop looking at him. The curly hair, grown slightly longer as she liked it, the faint stubble of a beard, which she didn't like. They turned and weaved their way through the scattered crowds in the busy terminal.

"The Tokyo airport was much nicer," she said, feeling very worldly.

"Gimpo is old," he said. "They're talking about building a new international airport. I think they start construction next year."

"You said you have a car?"

He nodded. "You won't believe the traffic here."

"Worse than Chicago?"

"Probably. Not so bad once we get where we're going." He passed an older couple pulling identical gray suitcases, and Gina hurried to keep up. "The hotel is about a ten-minute drive to the agency," Ian told her.

She noticed something in his hand. "What's that?"

He looked down. "A book I picked up at O'Hare." He showed her the cover: a dark figure with hooded eyes, almost engulfed by dark clouds. *Random Victim* was the title.

"That doesn't seem like something you'd read," she said.

"It's not, really." He tucked it under his arm. "I thought it might distract me, help kill time. Truth is, I keep carrying it around, but I can't get into it."

"Where's Carrie now?"

"Resting at the hotel. If we hurry, we can swing by and see Hana tonight. I told them we'd try to make it before eight o'clock."

"How far is it?"

He stopped at a restroom and looked at her. "It's twenty-two miles on the map, but it took me almost two hours. We still have to go through customs, but traffic should be better now."

"I'll hurry," she said, ducking inside. She caught a glimpse of herself in the mirror as she washed her hands. Hair mussed, face pasty, her sweater wrinkled and a dark spot she hadn't noticed on the sleeve. Quickly, she brushed her hair and swiped some color onto her lips.

Ian was waiting when she came out. A few more minutes of walking and one flight of steps and they were standing at the baggage carousel.

"It's a crazy city," he told her.

"Seoul?"

"No, I was talking about Cleveland."

She tightened her lips and her head tilted slightly, as she had seen her mother look at Ian many times.

"The traffic is chaotic," he continued. "It's a city of neighborhoods like Chicago, everything spread out but crowded together, too. Once in a while, you'll turn a corner and there's some of the ancient architecture. If we have time, we'll go to one of the palaces. There are several you can tour. Some have amazing gardens." He put his leg on the chrome frame, next to the rubber conveyer belt, which still wasn't moving. "Carrie and I saw Changdeokgung Palace and the secret garden there. We requested to take Hana. You're allowed to have an outing, but it's been so cold, they wouldn't let her out for the day."

Gina tapped Ian's leg and he put his foot back on the ground. "Chang what?" she asked.

"A palace from the Joseon Dynasty. It's interesting. They tried to build the whole thing to blend in with the nature already there, instead of taking over. Very organic."

"Hmm," Gina said. A man from her flight came and stood directly in front of her. She edged towards Ian.

The conveyer belt groaned to life; several people crowded forward.

"Let me get it," Ian said. "Tell me which one."

The bags begin to appear, unceremoniously dumped from an opening at the ceiling, tumbling down a ramp and settling onto the moving rubber. "Are we picking up Carrie first?" Gina asked.

"No," he said. "She'll stay at the hotel tonight."

She bit her lip. Her sweet brother, saddled with a difficult woman. They could've had the baby delivered to the airport, but it was Carrie who wanted to travel to the kid's homeland. They might have waited or looked into getting a local baby. All of it orchestrated by Carrie, and now something had gone wrong, and she rested at the hotel while Ian drove through hours of traffic in a rental he probably couldn't afford. Gina took a deep breath, made a vow to think positive thoughts.

"Is that it?" he asked.

She looked up and there it was: the bag she checked in Chicago, meekly approaching like some quiet miracle. The items inside flashed in her mind.

Ian reached over and hauled the suitcase up. His sweater rode up in the back and the plump sections of his lower back peeked out. Gina glanced around to see if anyone had noticed.

He placed the bag on the ground, pulled up the handle and looked at her. "Ready?"

The air was biting outside, the parking lot a short walk away. Gina's exposed ankles ached in the cold. The rental was a slate blue Hyundai. She pictured, again, her abandoned car, far away now.

"It's freezing," she said, rubbing her hands together as Ian loaded the suitcase into the trunk. He unlocked the doors and she ducked inside.

"I told you to dress like you weren't going anywhere," he said. "It's winter here, too. You need your boots."

"I couldn't wear them on the plane."

They left the airport and the land spread out. Snow coated the rises on either side of the highway; clouds turned to fog to a general grayness that covered everything. She looked around, her eyes settling on this or that, but nothing for long. A cold, winter day. A highway. Distant mountains. Snow. She waited for a long time, content to be next to him, waiting to see something new.

In time, she asked, "So what's happening, Ian?"

"I told you most of it already."

"You said I signed something to be a guardian?"

"Listen." He glanced at her, his round cheeks still red from the cold. "I knew you would freak out about that. Maybe I wasn't completely forthcoming when I had you sign the stuff. I didn't think it would be a big deal, and Carrie wanted to keep certain things personal."

"I wouldn't have freaked out," she said. "It makes sense. I'm the nearest relative."

"If you can help get us through what we need to do this week, we can always look into changing it later."

"Why?" she asked, hurt that maybe he'd changed his mind about having her be the guardian.

He closed his eyes for a moment, gathering himself. "We don't *have* to. I'm only saying, if you're not comfortable. But I want you to do it."

"I want to." Gina watched as they passed over a large body of water.

"That's the Han River," he said. "On the other side, the main part of Seoul. People once believed North Korea could flood South Korea if they wanted to, by releasing water from a dam further up."

"North Korea is the bad one."

"Right. South Koreans live in fear of them, and this was a big scare, one that eventually proved groundless."

"Like Y2K will be," she said.

Ian looked at her, his eyebrow cocked. "Yes, probably."

"My neighbor keeps telling me to stock up on water, canned food. What good is it to have a month's worth of paper towels if everyone has gone crazy looting?"

He chuckled. "You could bargain with household supplies, maybe. Cans of Campbell's instead of cash." He turned down the heater, which had warmed up the little car quickly.

"I don't see how computers can change so much," she said.

"The banks could shut down," Ian said. "What if you can't get your money?"

"I imagine they'd get it situated soon enough. This is America." She looked out the window. "Well, you know what I mean." She started to unbutton her coat. "Besides, it's not that much money."

Ian laughed at that, his shoulders bouncing and the curve of his belly pressing against the bottom of the steering wheel.

She missed his eyeglasses, the way they magnified his eyes but kept some of their vividness a secret. She and Ian had always shared limited vision, but now he saw clearly without any correction. When she pictured Ian in her mind, during the times they were apart, it was always with glasses, the round metal frames he'd always worn, and when they met up again, she was always startled to see him with an empty face. Six years had passed since his LASIK surgery, but Gina knew him a lifetime before that. Eventually, she supposed she'd get used to it.

"We're at the Seongbuk Holiday Inn," Ian said. It's in the mid-north part of the city. Like near north in Chicago, I guess."

"Sounds nice."

"You'll never get a feel for Seoul in a couple of days," he said. "I'm hoping we have time for the Namsan Tower. I've been told you can see the entire metro area from the top."

"Sometimes I get queasy with heights," she said.

"In the observation area, there are thousands of padlocks people have left. A tradition. Young couples—or even older ones, I guess. They profess their love for each other, write their names or something on the padlock, then clip it onto the bars or fences near the walkway. Like I said, there are thousands. Locks of love, they call them."

Through Gina's window, the scenery had thickened to include clusters of tall apartments, industrial, warehouse-type buildings, all the signs and clutter of city life. "Did you and Carrie do that?" she asked. "The padlock thing?"

Ian shook his head. "We haven't been there. She hasn't been feeling well."

Something about his tone made her look over.

"That's the rest of what I need to tell you." He paused, watching the road before them. "Carrie has MS. She's had it for years and most of that time, she's been in remission."

Gina watched his face. "MS—which one is that? Is it muscular something?"

His mouth tensed. "No, you're thinking of muscular dystrophy. This is multiple sclerosis. It has to do with the central nervous system."

"Oh."

"Your body's defense system attacks myelin, which is a fatty substance protecting your nerves. Usually, it's very manageable."

A memory flashed in her mind: Ian's description of his protein diet, Helen's funny comment about being a lion. The thought of your body acting against itself was a strange one.

"Is that why you have to adopt?" she asked.

"No, we didn't *have* to adopt," he said. "Women with MS can get pregnant and have perfectly healthy children. Carrie has to manage and monitor the disease. She takes a medication called Copaxone, which helps stop the progression."

Many questions raced through Gina's mind. Did he mean that Carrie would die at a young age? Was he leading up to tell her she was dying now? What did any of this have to do with the baby? She held her tongue and waited for the rest.

They left the interstate and came to a halt at a stoplight. Cars were packed onto the street and motorcycles weaved through. Ian released the steering wheel and looked over. "Sometimes you can have what's called an IPIR, a bad reaction to the medication, if you've accidentally hit a blood vessel instead of fat when you do the injection."

"You have to do injections?"

He nodded. "Carrie does them herself. You know, she was only twenty-four when she was diagnosed. She's dealt with this for a long time already."

Layers settled in Gina's mind, new realizations about her brother's wife.

"She had an IPIR on Thursday," he said.

"What is that again?"

"Immediate post-injection reaction. She couldn't breathe and started sweating. She said it feels like your whole body is swelling. It's awful." He rubbed his eyes roughly, trying to keep tears away.

Gina fought the urge to put her hand on his head. "Oh, Ian."

"This has only happened twice before," he said. "It can take hours or days to feel better and she still isn't feeling great."

The traffic lurched forward. They passed some sort of stadium, a long line of young people outside.

Ian's eyes met hers briefly. "We had a meeting with the agency on Friday and she couldn't go. They know about the MS, of course. We had to fill out a whole damn dossier on Carrie's health—doctor reports, testimonials on work attendance, even school records, although she never had it then." He took a breath. "The director is worried that Carrie's having some sort of relapse, and she wanted us to go back home and have a complete new set of medical reports drawn up."

"That's the person who has the baby?" she asked.

"Right. Well, there's no way in hell we're doing that. I can't even imagine, after everything we've been through." He turned onto a street with an empty lot on the corner, where two bundled men bent towards each other, their breaths steaming together in the frigid air.

"What happened?"

"With the interpreter, we went back and forth all day Friday. Had to get the agency's Kansas City central office on the line and get them involved. Finally on Saturday morning, they agreed to go through with the transfer and finalize the adoption, if the third guardian was present. That's you."

"And then you called me. Saturday here, but Friday night back home."

"Right."

They were silent for some time, both lost in their thoughts. The car made slow progress, crawling through stoplights with the heavy traffic. Gina watched the city until Ian parked the car next to a gray building with an undulating cement facade and a bright blue banner stretching the length of the uppermost sections. Construction cranes hovered at the top, and a covered tunnel arched across the busy street for pedestrians. The Holiday Inn sign was the same logo as in the States, green and white and cursive. The writing on the blue banner was foreign.

Ian turned off the engine and leaned back. "Honestly, I think this is all out-of-the-ordinary. The Korean agency is in some chaos right now. Our adoption is the last one slated on their calendar before a three-week break. Kansas City told us that. They're moving locations, somewhere closer to the city. Until that's done, they're halting finalizations."

"I don't understand," Gina said.

"They want this adoption to go through because it would mean a lot of red tape and hassle if it didn't. So, they're trying to work with us and get it done."

"That's good, right?"

He smiled, a watered-down version of his usual. "Yes." His eyes flickered up. "This is our hotel. I booked you a room down the hall from ours. Would you mind waiting in the car while I check on Carrie? I'd have you come up, but I'm not sure how she's doing. We'll get you checked in when we get back from the agency."

"That's fine." She watched as he made his way to the revolving door of the hotel, watched him hunker down and press through. The chill crept in; she heard a faint whistle of air coming through some opening in the back of the car. She pulled her coat more tightly around her. The hotel seemed worn down and well used, not unlike certain buildings in Berwyn. Across the street, squat buildings were grouped, one next to the other, plastered with bright-colored signs and lit from within by fluorescents. Shops, restaurants, services. She had hardly noticed the city growing dark around her, but now she saw the flickering lights interspersed throughout the small parking lot, the layers of illumination squashed between concrete in the larger parking structure adjacent to the hotel.

She looked at her watch, which she had changed when the flight attendants announced the local time. Just after 7:15. It must have been dark for some time; why hadn't she noticed? Her breath was visible now, the car probably slightly warmer than the climate outside. Throughout everything, she hadn't given much thought to the baby. Concerned about Ian and the great distance, then completely preoccupied with her own last-minute trip, the idea of what would happen once the baby was home had never occurred to her more than in passing. But things would change, she realized now. They already had.

Ian emerged from the building, his hands shoved into the pockets of his coat. As he got closer, she heard a slight tinkling, growing louder: the keys. He opened the door and all at once, his presence overtook the small interior. A rush of warm air, the bulk of him, his musky smell.

"She's feeling much better," he said. "Got a lot of rest and ordered room service."

"I'm so glad," Gina said.

"Oh, my God," he said, fully looking at her.

Arms locked across her chest, shoulders hunched, she stared back. "What?"

"You're freezing!" He put the key in and started the engine. "Why didn't you come inside?"

"You told me to wait here," she said, embarrassed by his tone. "I didn't mind."

He turned the heater until it was blasting cold air at the highest setting. "This warms up quickly."

"It's fine, Ian. Really."

"Is your suitcase locked?"

"Why?"

"I'm going to bring it to the backseat so you can get your boots."

"There's no lock," she said.

"Do you have a scarf in there?"

"Yes, my green one."

"Okay, hold on."

And he went back into the cold night and walked around to the back of the car. Gina turned and watched him. He came back to press the button to unlock the trunk—he had forgotten that—and watching him make the second trip brought a wave of guilt to her. But she felt grateful, touched by his simple act, his desire to take care of her. Tears filled her eyes, but she blinked them back.

While the heater began to replace cold air with hot, Ian opened her suitcase on the back seat. She rifled through the tiers of clothing and found her leather ankle boots. In a zippered pouch next to her undergarments was the green wool scarf. Ian was right. She felt much better after the scarf was wrapped around her neck, the boots zipped and tucked under her pants.

Outside the cocoon of the car, Seoul twinkled and pulsed around them. Traffic had lessened as people settled for the night. Another Monday to them— a day at work, dinner with families or friends, a night of television. Lives not unlike her own, probably. She wondered how Mr. Seutter had taken the news of her absence. Probably Amanda Blevin had stepped in to help with phone calls and messages, with mail and the occasional letters he liked to dictate the old-fashioned way, into a machine they ordered from Ohio. She stifled a grin, imagining Nehra's reaction to her absence. Nehra, who didn't even think Gina could drive into the city to save her brother after Y2K.

Some of the tension had left Ian's face, and he looked more like himself. A song pulsed through her head, the commercial, the dancing young people spinning and turning, throwing each other through the air.

Baby, baby, it looks like it's gonna hail. You gotta jump, jive, and then you wail. You gotta jump, jive, and then you wail.

Settling once again into the car and growing warmer by the moment, Gina watched through the moving screen of the window as the city passed in scenes. Here, a busy gas station, there a restaurant and a petite waitress balancing a large tray on her shoulder. Car lights blinking and staring, blackening sky meeting the horizon of buildings. Her brother, real and fully formed beside her.

19

The adoption agency was on a sloping hill, on a street that ended with a fork in the road. One path continued up the hill and the other flattened and veered to the left. At the place where the two choices converged, a triangular, brick building jutted up from the asphalt. The side overlooking the street was glass from ground to roof, a convex series of windows that reflected Ian's rented Hyundai and everything behind it. This building was not the agency.

"We have to park here and walk down," Ian said. "You can see the street is narrow. Some of these bigger doors are garages so you can't park in front of them."

Gina looked at the motley assortment of structures lining the road. A brick, three-story building, the windows blocked with blinds, was followed by a bi-level, wooden house with a long balcony, then a big, windowless box, concrete but painted to look like cobblestone, with a yellow sign anchored to the top corner. A business, probably. Wherever possible, small cars were parked, some facing up the street and others down; frequently, their headlights almost touching.

They got out of the car and began walking.

"I talked to Deborah yesterday," Ian told her.

She was surprised but didn't say so. According to their sister, Ian never made much effort where she was concerned. Gina couldn't exactly blame him. Her siblings' lives were so different, with the disparity between their ages and Deborah being gone for so long. Often, their only knowledge of each other came through Gina. She sometimes wondered if they would ever speak again if something happened to her.

"She was worried about you," he said.

"About me? Why?"

Ian looked at her with mischievous eyes that made him seem very young. "She thought we'd lose you in the Tokyo airport."

Gina snorted.

"And she wasn't sure how you'd do, you know, being away from home."

"She likes to think of me a certain way."

"She feels left out, I think." Ian kicked a bottle cap with his tan, stiff-toed boots. "It must be hard for her, living out there with us in Berwyn."

"That was her choice."

"Doesn't change the way she feels now."

Gina's ears were burning from the cold. "How much farther?"

"Not far."

They passed through a band of aroma—meat cooking, some sort of spice. Gina's stomach turned over. She tried to figure out what time it was back home and when she'd had her last meal, but everything was so confused, what with the extra snacks on the airplane and the short intervals of sleep. "I forgot my vitamins," she said.

Ian's nose was red from the cold. "You still take, what, a multi-vitamin?"

"And calcium," she said. "In the winter, extra D."

"I think you'll survive a few days without them. It's not like you're going to catch rickets or something."

He stopped in front of an iron gate, locked with a huge brass padlock. To the left of the gate was a button, almost hidden between the bricks that formed the first of several balusters. The entire building was surrounded in iron and the building itself, also grayish brick, stood six feet back from the fence.

"This is it," Ian said. "Mostly they have administrative offices inside, but there is one section for children. See, the babies go to foster homes when they're born. That's one thing we really liked about their program. There aren't rows of cribs with only a nurse or two to look after them. From the day she was born four months ago, Hana's been with a woman named Ho Sook. We met her the other day."

"Does she get paid for that?" Gina asked.

"Yes, but she still loved the baby. You could tell."

"I was only wondering."

"Carrie's worried," he said. "Hana's been here for three nights now, instead of only one as planned. I think she's getting plenty of attention, but it's not like having a foster mother." He pushed the button, and a faint buzzing could be heard from within.

The house seemed dark and quiet. "Are you sure they're expecting us?" she asked.

"I spoke to them." He took his hands from his pockets and rubbed them together. "You look nice," he said. "Very respectable."

Gina watched the darkened windows for any signs of life. Next to her, Ian had grown quiet. He seemed nervous, as nervous as she'd ever seen him.

"Do you remember when that kid stole your bicycle?" she asked.

"What made you think of that?"

"Because of the way you look right now. Remember, he inspected the bike right in front of you."

Ian smiled. "He even told me how much he could get for it."

"And then he came and stole it from the side yard. And you knew right away who'd done it."

He pushed the button again, shuffled on his feet.

"Mom made you go with her to get it," she said.

"So, embarrassing," he said. "His parents were there. He had hidden the bike down the street from his house. I can't believe she dragged me along."

"Would you've rather lost your bike?"

"Maybe."

A small figure appeared on the porch. The woman, short and bundled in long layers of clothing, shuffled towards them, stepping down until she stood on the other side of the gate. "Door already locked," she said.

"Hello," Ian said. "Yes, but I spoke to Mrs. Kim. She said if we came before eight o'clock, we could see the baby."

"Baby sleep," the woman said.

Gina glanced at her watch: 7:53. "Maybe we can come back—"

Ian gripped the iron bars. "Please, could we look at her? My sister traveled from the United States."

The woman looked Gina over. "Baby sleep," she said again.

"We won't wake her," he said. "Please. I promised my wife."

Gina tried to put a pleasant look on her face. The woman sighed, a big gesture, the layers of her long gown, or dress, or whatever it was, rising and settling again. "Wait." She climbed the steps to the porch and disappeared behind the door. When she came back, she handed a key to Ian. "You lock," she said, meaning *unlock*.

Inside, two desks faced each other next to a tray holding a fax machine and stacks of paper. File cabinets ran along one side of the room and nearby, a battered sofa was pushed against another wall. A narrow opening was lit in a soft glow; the diminutive woman led them towards it.

The hallway was close, with a low ceiling and a darker path worn down the center. They passed two closed doors and halted at the third. The door creaked a bit as it opened. Gina noticed first a nightlight, a yellow cow endlessly jumping over a crescent moon, the plastic tilted a bit so that the cow seemed to be diving directly downwards. Ian stepped forward and she followed him. The room had an intense, encompassing smell: sweet and sour, powder and urine, dry linens, and dampened wood. All of it at once.

Gina stepped up to the crib, placed her hands on the cold metal frame next to Ian's.

Hana slept on her stomach, surrounded by a mountain range of blankets. One silken hem was close to her face, rippling slightly when her breath expelled, changing color in the dim light when she inhaled. Her legs were splayed out and bent, accordion-like, her feet almost touching in tiny, white socks. Doughy and creaseless, her hands were clenched into fists, each laid alongside her head. But it was her face that made Gina's breath catch. Eyelashes like shiny, black threads, her flawlessly formed mouth, her skin like some painted surface, perfect and smooth. The cap of black hair, straight and fine, curling the slightest bit behind her ear. Gina reached over and placed her hand on the baby's back, where it fit perfectly in the groove above the padded diaper. She could feel the rise and fall of her breaths, the rapid testimony of her little heart.

"Goodness, Ian," she said, her voice cracking. "I couldn't imagine—"

"Isn't she beautiful?" He edged closer to Gina, his hip against her side as they looked down.

Gina tried again. "I never thought—"

She could hear Ian's breathing, measured and calm, in the close room. And the distant cars and a clock somewhere, measuring moments. She kept her hand on the baby's warm back.

The old woman lingered in the shadows but after a short time, she stepped to the end of the crib. Her demeanor had softened; her knobby hands were folded as one in front of her. "You ready?" she whispered.

Slowly, they followed her out. They made the trek back up the hill. The night was colder now, frosty, the wind reduced to a slight breeze. Ian stepped to the passenger side and let Gina in first. The car was frigid again. She folded her arms across her chest and tucked her hands under the armpits of her coat.

Once they'd started driving, Ian took a deep breath. "I don't know what we'll do if this doesn't happen," he said.

"It will," she said.

"The minute we found out about Hana and saw her photo, it's like she was immediately ours."

"She's perfect," Gina said.

"And to be here, to see her and hold her." He blinked rapidly. "I have no idea what it would do to Carrie if we left without her."

"Stop thinking about it." She patted his arm. "They want to see me, make sure I'm able to help you?"

"Yes. They may ask some questions."

"About what?"

"About Carrie's MS, what you know about it."

"But I didn't know."

His hands squeaked on the steering wheel as he turned onto a busy, three-lane road. "I think maybe you should say you did. I don't want them thinking we were hiding anything from them, from our family."

"Why *didn't* you tell me?"

He shrugged. "She doesn't want people to treat her differently, and she doesn't want to talk about it all the time. When you have a condition like that, people seem to think it consumes every moment of your existence. And while in a way, it does, we try very hard not to let it. You can't imagine what it's like at her parents' house. 'How are you feeling Carrie? Oh, let me get that, Carrie, you shouldn't be lifting that.'"

"I see."

"Also, she didn't want anyone in our family thinking she wasn't good enough, that I was making a mistake marrying her."

"I wouldn't have—"

Ian put his hand up. "I'm only telling you what she thought. You know, it really hasn't affected anything for us, not until now."

"I'm glad you called me, Ian. I'm glad I'm here with you. You said she's feeling better today?"

"Yeah."

They drove along, their faces colored by the lighted, foreign signs, the greens, yellows and reds, the series of slanted lines and the occasional loop, all of it seeming impossible and undecipherable, but the buildings underneath recognizable for what they contained and by the glimpses of the people inside. Gina thought about what it would be like to live in Seoul, to make your way without the benefit of clear communication and certain signals. It would make things difficult, but exciting. Retrieving something from the grocery store would feel like a small triumph.

"I read something once," her brother said, "about what it feels like to become an orphan."

Gina's head snapped towards him.

"We hold onto our parents because their presence allows us to revisit childhood. Around them, we can still feel like kids—even if it's in some altered, half-satisfying way. The loss of them is the final sundering."

She asked, quietly, "What's sundering?"

"Breaking free."

At the end of a winding and car-packed street, the Holiday Inn stood, its blue banner lit with a string of lights. They stopped at the intersection, waiting.

"When Mom died, did you feel like an orphan, Meema?"

The streetlight, still red, pulsing. "I don't know," she said.

"Having Hana has alleviated that feeling a little already," he said. "At least for me. You know, I'd never tell Carrie this, but the first adoption, the baby boy, I never thought it would work out."

She pressed a hand to her cheek, felt the coldness in her fingers. "You didn't?"

"We couldn't agree on a name, not really, and when we met the birth mother, something in her eyes—"

"I know you were disappointed," Gina said.

He turned towards her, his face expanding into a grin. "I haven't told you her middle name."

"Carrie's?"

He rolled his eyes. "No, the baby's."

"What is it?"

"Hee Young," he said. "It means 'eternal' and 'pleasure and prosperity.' I wanted to pick names that started with an 'h,' for Mom."

"For Daddy too," she said. "That's nice."

"In Korean culture, expectant mothers are only allowed to see beautiful things, so the baby will see what she does. The mother eats warm foods, because it's believed babies are cold. You should see how they pile clothes on Hana, layer after layer."

"And then you have Deborah," Gina said, "who never put socks on her kids, even in the winter. 'It's California,' she'd say."

Ian shrugged. "I didn't see the boys much when they were little."

"You were still young yourself."

"The mother-in-law plays a big role here," he said. "When a baby's born, she pretty much takes over."

"Mom would have done that."

At the hotel, Ian maneuvered the car into the larger parking structure, after finding no spaces in the small lot. They wound their way up, one level to the next. On the fifth, he pulled into a spot and turned off the engine. "If everything goes well tomorrow, Carrie and I would like to have a ceremony after the courthouse. Our flight Wednesday leaves in the afternoon."

"Ceremony?"

"It's a custom to pray avalokiteshvara for the baby, both before the birth and to protect the child against natural disasters. The women at the agency helped us find someone who can come and do this for Hana."

"Okay."

"I know sometimes you don't see the value in things like that—"

She opened her mouth to interrupt but he continued.

"—but the thing is, Meema, these ceremonies mark something important." He pulled the keys from the ignition. "You can't have too many people rooting for you, can you?"

"Ian, I think it sounds great."

"Good. Because we'll have a big party for her first birthday too, with lots of Korean stuff going on." He faced her. "You must be hungry."

"I'm fine."

"There's a restaurant in the hotel. Very limited menu, but you can get a hamburger."

"That sounds perfect."

They parted in the lobby after Ian got her room key at the front desk. Gina's room, 423, was on the fourth floor, down and across the hall from theirs. Ian wrote 416 on the cardboard folder that housed her key, which really wasn't a key at all but a credit card with a photo of the hotel on the front. The man at the front desk took charge of Gina's suitcase and promised to deliver it directly to her room. Ian said they'd meet for breakfast at eight o'clock then head to the agency to take care of things. He apologized for not joining her in the restaurant, but with the trip to the airport, he'd been away from Carrie most of the day. Gina said she understood.

The restaurant wasn't large, about fifteen tables, three of them occupied. The television screen over the bar was set to a news station. The waitress took her to a small table near the entrance, where she could look out over the lobby. Gina was relieved to see that the menu was subtitled in English. At times, the translation was questionable, but it was good enough. She pointed to a drink called a Cherry Bomb—vodka, 7-Up, grenadine—and to a photo of a hamburger and fries.

She had set her purse on the ground between her feet, but she brought it up now to the table. She thought about the manila envelope buried at the bottom, the report filed by Dr. Trainor. She had carried it around for so long.

The drink came, perfectly cold, sweet but not overly so. Gina hadn't realized how thirsty she was. On the television screen over the bar, an image of a delivery truck turned onto its side and engulfed in flames. The fire was greedy, almost angry in the way it whipped itself up in the wind. A woman was being interviewed; her face was unmoving. The camera went back to the truck, something white spilling from the back. Linens, boxes, perhaps boxes of linens. A shift of the camera angle and the truck cab was visible, flames billowing around the black steering wheel. Behind, the busy highway, cars pressing forward, the asphalt glistening. Firemen wrestling with the powerful hose. Again, the woman, clutching a teenaged boy against her chest. A trio of men in suits, the middle one behind a podium. The truck, incapacitated, unmoving. And the story, without benefit of sound or language, began to emerge. A man, maybe a victim, maybe a culprit. The woman, caught unaware. A tragedy. Gina looked around the quiet restaurant and sipped her drink. She held off fatigue for a good while longer and by the time she had finished her meal and signed the check, the restaurant was filling up and becoming loud.

20

The alarm clock rang at 7:00, its trill foreign although it was a Sony, a brand Gina recognized. It took her eyes several moments to focus on the room. The waffle print of the dark green bedspread, the watercolor of a forest on the opposite wall. Remarkably, she had slept like a rock. She'd expected to have issues with the temperature, the stiff pillow, the street sounds, but the last thing she remembered was pulling her feet from the fleece-lined slippers which sat nearby, their blue bows lined up. She gazed at them over the side of the bed, thinking what a nice and practical gift they were.

She leaned back against the pillow, which had softened up a bit during the night. Her thoughts turned to the contents of her suitcase, the slacks, blouses and shoes, and which combination would be best for what needed to be done.

The coffee maker, like the alarm clock, was familiar and easy to operate. She brewed a cup of regular and stepped into the bathroom. Here, the Holiday Inn had done themselves proud. Gray tiles reached from the floor to waist-high then lightened to white. They reached all the way to the ceiling. The sink was metal and elevated on the counter, with a border of pale blue tiles and a faucet that reminded her of a crane's elegant neck. She decided she'd remodel her bathroom at home to look like this one.

In the shower, she went about her usual routine, using the smaller containers she had packed in a gallon-sized Ziploc bag. Even the showerhead seemed sumptuous and stylish, with a round head and countless apertures. The water fell like soft rain. She lingered, washing with the hotel's body wash twice, letting the water grow hotter and hotter. When she turned the stream off, she heard a faint buzzing through the wall. By the time it dawned on her that it might be the telephone, by the time she had wrapped a towel around her hair and one around her body and her feet had left a wet path on the carpet, it had stopped ringing. She found the cardboard folder with Ian's room number and followed the directions on the telephone.

His voice was husky. "Hello?"

"Ian, did you call me?"

"Yeah." He coughed a bit, clearing his throat. "First, good morning."

"Good morning."

"Sleep well?"

"I did," she said. "It's a very comfortable room. I wish you'd let me pay. You've got expenses coming up."

"Enough," he said, but his voice was playful. "We're paying. Listen, I've got a great feeling this morning. Have you seen the sun?"

"The sun?"

"You know, big white object, illuminates the earth?"

"Funny," she said. "I had a shower. I haven't looked."

"The point is, it's a beautiful day," he said. "Carrie's back to her old, ornery self—" Here, Carrie's voice and a shuffling, as if she had thrown something at him. "And my sister's here. All of us in Seoul, Korea, to pick up our daughter."

"Have you been drinking?" Gina asked.

"Now you're the funny one," he said. "We slept in a little. It's the first good night's sleep I've had here." He crumpled something, a paper. "The agency opens at 9:30. As long as we're on the road by 9:15, it's fine. But I don't think we'll make it down for breakfast at 8:00. Why don't you come to our room? Carrie's waiting until her father gets home from work. She wants to call and give them an update. Then we can head down together."

"Give me twenty minutes," she said.

Shortly afterwards, Gina stood in the hall outside Ian and Carrie's room. Another artificial and strange setting, with its series of doors and the loud, multi-colored carpet. The door swung open, and Carrie stood in a pair of black slacks and a lace-trimmed blouse. Gina had forgotten how petite she was, how pretty.

Carrie rushed forward and embraced her. "It's so nice to see you."

Gina leaned in, patting Carrie's slender shoulders.

"I haven't been able to reach my parents, but I'll try one more time."

Gina stepped into their hotel room, a duplicate of hers, flipped. The same green bedspread, the same paintings. Ian's suitcase was open on a luggage stand; she knew it was his because of the disarray inside. In the closet, Carrie's clothes were hung neatly.

"I hope you were able to sleep?" Carrie asked. "I know it's hard sometimes when you're away from home." She brought the desk chair over. "Did Ian snore when he was a kid?"

"I don't think so."

"He does now. I wear earplugs." She patted the chair.

Gina hung her purse from the back of the chair and sat down. "I told Ian I slept very well. Exhausted, I guess." She looked around. "Where is he?"

Carrie tucked her hair behind one ear and sat on the bed. "I had to send him to the store. I needed some, well, some feminine products."

"Oh."

"My luck hasn't been very good on this trip, but I refuse to take it as an omen."

Gina shook her head. "You shouldn't. It doesn't mean anything."

"Ian told you about my MS and the IPIR?"

"Yes."

Her chin jutted forward. "I'm glad you know, Gina. I've been very fortunate, really." She smiled. "I hope you weren't offended we never mentioned it before."

"No, it's your business."

She clapped her hands together. "Let me try my mom and dad one more time. Ian said he'd meet us in the restaurant, and we should go ahead and order his breakfast."

"Pancakes?" Gina asked.

Carrie laughed. "He's trying to stick to this latest diet, even though he couldn't bring the food with him. He wants to be healthy, especially now. I'm so proud of him." She stepped over to the phone, which sat on the nightstand alongside a glass of water, an alarm clock, and a small grouping of medicine bottles.

Gina looked away, not wanting to be nosy.

The telephone buttons made a small clicking sound as Carrie pushed them; it seemed like quite a lot of numbers. Carrie tapped her foot as she waited for the connection. "Hi Mommy, hi Dad. Don't worry, everything's fine. Just wanted to talk before we head over to the agency. Gina's here now, thank God, and we should be able to do the paperwork and get clearance. I think we may be able to finalize this afternoon." She listened for a few moments, then her voice grew unsteady. "Thanks. I love you guys. I'll call you later today, hopefully with good news."

She hung up the phone and turned around. "I was hoping to reach them. I'm so nervous."

"Ian seems to think there won't be a problem," Gina said.

"I know, I know." She put her hands up in surrender. "Hard not to believe in him, isn't it? You can get swept up."

"Yes," she said, smiling.

Carrie moved back to the bed and sat across from Gina. "There are a few things I want to say to you, and I'm glad we have this chance. I wasn't sure if we would, with everything going on."

Gina squirmed in her chair and started to get up. "It's a big day."

"Wait," Carrie said. "Let me, please."

She folded her hands on her lap.

"I told you about my brothers, right?"

Gina nodded.

"Chet is three years younger than me, and Chris is six years younger. Leave it to my parents to have three kids, each one three years apart. They're very orderly people." She clasped the greenish bracelet around her wrist, turning it this way and that. "I always felt a certain responsibility towards my brothers, not only at home but when we were out in the world. And when I left the house, I had an overwhelming sense of guilt. I guess it's egotistical in a way, but I felt like I was abandoning them. Of course, I wasn't their parent, and they had our parents who are quite caring and responsible."

"What does this—"

"I'm trying to say is that I've always understood your relationship with Ian, and I've never been threatened by it. I appreciate the way you watch over him and worry. I really do."

Gina looked at her. "Ian's a grown man. Things change."

"They change, yes." Carrie crossed her arms. "I also want to apologize for that night at the loft, for the things I said."

"No, there's no reason." She turned her legs to stand.

"I had no right to tell you anything about your life, Gina. I was so sad about losing the first baby." She sighed. "You were right. I was feeling sorry for myself and thinking no one could possibly understand."

The curtain was pulled back from the window, sunlight streaming across the bedspread. "I understand," she said. "You had plans. Even in that short time, you had started to make plans."

Carrie nodded. "And even though we never met him, never got to hold him—even so, it was a loss, at least to me."

"There's nothing to do about it now."

"What I'm saying is, if you felt the loss, then it was a loss."

"But to wallow in it." Gina shook her head. "To carry it around for years, when it wasn't even—" The chair was cutting into her back now, the bars of the seatback pressing in, making her sit straight to alleviate the pressure.

"You were young, Gina."

"I'm not sure what to think," she said. "He told me—Dr. Trainor—he said there was a problem with my heart. And the exam, it was painful, I was sure he'd done something. Then later, the bleeding—"

Carrie put her hands on Gina's knees. "But to do that in his office and then send you home? It would've been more than that, can you see?"

Tears flooded Gina's eyes and when she took off her glasses, everything blurred. "For a long time, I thought I had a hole in my heart. That's what it felt like."

Carrie nodded, crying herself now, the tears falling and absorbing immediately into her black slacks. "I know." She jumped up and found a box of tissues in the bathroom, handing one to Gina and keeping one to dab her own eyes. "I think the last thing people should judge is someone else's suffering. It doesn't really matter now, does it, Gina? You've felt this loss for so long, that's the important thing."

"But wasn't I stupid?"

"No."

They faced each other, sniffling and wiping.

Gina looked again at the window, at the covered walkway that traversed the busy street below, at the steam issuing from a distant building like an offering to the brilliant blue sky. She would leave it in Korea, she decided. The pain, which she had nurtured close to her heart, she would leave it here and go home alone. She really sobbed then, her voice making sounds she was ashamed to hear but couldn't stop. Carrie started to get up to come to her but stayed where she was, and Gina appreciated her more in that moment than she ever had. She didn't want anyone touching her, not right then. It all rushed back—her mother, her father, all the losses big and small—like a flood, a torrent, and then it quietly drained away. They both took fresh tissues and were in the process of clearing their noses when the door was unlocked, and Ian came in.

At the sight of them, his mouth opened and closed. He let the door shut softly behind him and stood there, one hand dangling at his side and the other clutching a plastic grocery bag.

Carrie looked up at him, then back at Gina. They both laughed a small, soggy laugh, embarrassed, exposed.

"I've made an important decision," Ian said. Crossing the room, he threw the bag onto the bed. "I'm ordering champagne."

"It's eight-thirty in the morning," Carrie said, sniffling.

"And it's a big day," he said. "We're going to celebrate early, we're going to see our daughter, then we're going to celebrate again." He looked back and forth between them, his curly hair all messy, his beard fuller than the day before. "Oh, and I'm going to have pancakes. Just this once."

Gina stood up and took her purse from the chair. "Let's go," she said, still dabbing at her nose with the tissue. "I know from experience, if you get between Ian and pancakes, you're bound to get trampled."

He swung his arm and she ducked under it. She went to stand by the door. Her throat ached, but she'd press it down and put on a brave face for Ian and Carrie. This was their day and she'd have plenty of time for the rest later.

21

Seoul was bright and clear, everything in the pastel, comic-book colors of morning. The final layers of night's cold lingered in pockets as the sun rose. Gina sat in the back of Ian's rental car, her sensible shoes tucked underneath the front seat. Maybe Ian was right. It would be a good day.

The streets had a different energy than the night before. A morning buzz, people bustling with purpose, coats open and voices loud. A truck driver waited at the corner and waved for Ian to go through the intersection first. His face spread into a smile, and he nodded, ever so slightly, from his high position in the truck's cab.

The car left the broad roads and weaved through narrower ones, climbing at last the small hill with the triangular building at its peak. Ian had been chatting throughout the drive, about his breakfast, the hotel, the weather—anything that occurred to him, but Gina and Carrie had answered with little more than nods and the occasional single-syllable agreement.

Ian maneuvered the car into a cramped spot near the concrete building with grayish squares painted to resemble cobblestone. "Here we are," he said. They each opened a door and stepped out. Slowly, they trudged towards the adoption agency.

At the iron gate, the padlock had been removed. As Ian reached over to pull the latch, the old woman who'd let them in to see Hana the night before appeared on the front step. She wore the same long garment, but her demeanor was much more welcoming. Like an elfish character from a movie, with her wizened face and surprising spryness, she reminded Gina for a moment of Mrs. Spark.

"Come." She beckoned them forward and led them into the small office. Scurrying around, she pushed two chairs together, motioned for Carrie and Gina to sit, and disappeared around a corner.

The morning brightness made the dinginess of the space more apparent than it had been at night. The desks were old and scuffed, and the well-worn, green floor tile was darkened by years of ground-in soot. But everything was orderly and maintained, that much Gina could tell.

The old woman returned with another woman.

"Mrs. Kim," Ian said.

She shook his hand and held it, nodding slightly. When she let go, Ian turned towards Gina. "Mrs. Kim," he said, "this is my sister."

"Oh, yes." She grabbed Gina's hand and pressed it. Her hands were warm and smooth. "Welcome."

"Thank you," Gina said.

Mrs. Kim was younger than the older woman, but it was difficult to say how much. Her hair was pulled back into a small bun, and she wore a navy blue jacket over a long, patterned skirt. She motioned to the older woman, who left the room immediately. "Some tea," she explained.

Carrie stood up and came forward. "Mrs. Kim, so nice to see you."

Mrs. Kim's eyes narrowed a bit as she looked her over. "Yes, nice." Then something softened in her expression, as though Carrie had passed a test. "You sit," she instructed, and Carrie returned to her chair.

Gina was expecting a different sort of person to head the agency, her ideas of business leaders coming from her own work experiences. She had pictured Mrs. Kim in clicking high heels, with perfectly coiffed hair and a leather satchel. But these were silly expectations. This was a different world.

Mrs. Kim wheeled one of the office chairs over for Ian and sat behind the other desk. The old woman brought tea in a flowered porcelain teapot, with cups so dainty Gina had a hard time holding hers at first. The tea was terrible, even with two spoons of sugar, but she sipped it anyway. There were bland, almond-flavored pastries, shaped like crescents and fanned out on a matching plate.

They ate and drank and looked nervously at each other.

"Waiting for the translator?" Ian asked.

"Yes," Mrs. Kim said. "He call, say traffic very bad."

"How is the baby this morning?" Carrie asked. Her face was so anxious and overtaken with longing, Gina had to look away.

"She eat rice food this morning," Mrs. Kim said. "Sleep now."

The door creaked open and a neatly dressed young man with longish hair came in. He nodded and hung his coat on a rack near the door. Gina still had hers on and she felt stuck with it now. Her back was damp with sweat.

The older woman cleared away the tea necessities and they got down to business. The young man was the translator, and he went through a series of papers. For each one, he'd spend a moment conferring with Mrs. Kim then explain the form in English. Afterwards, Ian would sign, and Carrie would follow suit. They went through this process for several forms. There didn't seem to be much for Gina to do and she wished she could walk down the hallway and see Hana again. She thought about the baby's black hair, with the curling tendril behind her ear, the smooth skin and perfectly drawn features.

"Gina?" Ian was glaring across the room.

"What? Sorry." She stood up.

Mrs. Kim waved her hands. "No, please to sit. Questions for you now."

The translator had another sheaf of papers, which he pulled from a black folder. He made a series of marks as he asked Gina her name, her age, her relation to the couple. Was she of sound mind and body? Did she have adequate housing? Other children? Housemates? What was her employment history? Working hours? Income?

She answered the questions easily, feeling more capable as they went along, as she watched Ian and felt again like the older sister, the responsible one. When she had finished the questions, which ended with an encouraging smile from Mrs. Kim, Gina leaned back in her chair. Thoughts of her father crept in. It had never occurred to her to consider the responsibilities he must have felt. A wife, three children, a job he never loved. Everything required of him, every day. What's that saying about success and how so much depends on showing up? She must have seemed very enigmatic to him. A young girl with no clear purpose, possibly in trouble. Was it feasible for any of them to fully understand the other? Her father had a certain comfort with Deborah and as much as this had hurt Gina in the past, she understood it now. Each person incomprehensible, each needed and appreciated in different ways. The singular understanding, the need she felt for Ian was perhaps what their father felt for Deborah and now what Ian feels for Carrie and maybe, for Hana. And, so what? All of it was love.

They drove in two cars to the local courthouse. The translator, Mrs. Kim, and Hana in one car, Gina, Carrie, and Ian following behind. Another room, another set of papers. Carrie dabbing quiet tears, Ian's large hand on the back of his wife's neck, Gina standing behind them as they signed the final paper. Another caravan to a restaurant, this time the baby in the car seat beside Carrie, Gina craning her neck from the front and admonishing Ian to watch the road before he killed them all. In addition to the car seat borrowed from the agency, Hana had a few belongings: a decorated rucksack, two sets of clothing and a thin, impractical blanket, embroidered like the bag by the foster mother who took care of her for several months.

The restaurant was dark, trimmed with red enamel wording under the ceiling, around the entire room—a continuous, unknowable pronouncement. Ian was ecstatic. He shook hands with the manager and brought back the menu. Mrs. Kim pointed out dishes and when the waitress, a young girl in a pale pink smock arrived, Ian deferred to the agency head.

Carrie sat across from Gina with Hana in her lap. She couldn't quite get settled with the baby, couldn't decide whether she wanted her seated, face outward, or turned and propped on her shoulder. Frequently, she leaned down and smelled the baby's hair.

"Have you had Korean food?" the translator asked.

Gina shook her head.

"We tried a place in Chicago," Ian said. "And of course, we've been enjoying new things this week."

Carrie's face was pale, voracious, and yet she said, "I'm not really hungry."

"You'll eat," Ian told her. Then he reached over and gently took the baby's hand. He brought it to his lips and made a loud quacking noise that startled them all.

"Ian!" Carrie put her forearm across Hana's chest. "You'll make her cry."

"She's laughing," Gina said.

They all looked at the baby, whose silent convulsions at that moment exploded to laughter. And within moments, they were all laughing, and laughing some more, the wave of it rising and falling then rising again, until Gina had to wipe tears from her eyes.

Ian beamed. "See, honey, she has my sense of humor."

The waitress appeared with a tray and began to arrange a surprising number of small dishes on the table.

"Look at this, Hana," Carrie said. "All of this because of you. Ian, hold her for a minute while I make a bottle."

The waitress brought a few more items and somehow found room on the crowded table for them. Nothing was identifiable to Gina. Everything was yellowish or red, some of it cut into strange shapes, some of it covered in sauce. Two of the entrees were still bubbling with heat. "I hope someone will tell us what everything is," she said. "I mean, it looks great."

The translator began to point and explain each dish. He bent at the waist, hovering over the table, his greenish pants pinched at the groin from sitting.

Gina tried to pay attention but afterwards, could remember only two items: *modum jeom*, which he said was assorted fried items—fish, vegetables, meat—and *kimchi stew*, made with kimchi (whatever that was) and pork. She watched how the others ate and tried to be a good sport about trying most of the dishes on the table. But many were spicy and strange and often, she couldn't identify what type of meat or fish she was eating.

Carrie fed the baby her bottle and took occasional bites from her own plate. Towards the end of the lunch, Hana fell asleep.

Ian chatted with the translator and Mrs. Kim throughout, his charm trumping the difficulties of language. By the end of the meal, he had won them over, as he always did. The waitress brought the check and one last plate.

"Rice cakes," Mrs. Kim said, nodding.

Ian's chair scraped across the floor as he stood up. He motioned to the translator. "Jung-Yoon has agreed to lead us in a traditional blessing for Hana. According to Korean tradition, if an infant survived the first one hundred days, the family would have a celebration, to give thanks and make offerings." He looked at Carrie. "We hope to follow some traditions and make our own as well. Because we're very happy to have Hana with us, as part of our family from now on."

The translator took a piece of paper from his pocket and read for a short while. Gina bowed her head although she wasn't sure that was the appropriate thing to do. When he finished, she looked up.

Ian prodded Carrie, who was staring at the sleeping baby. "Oh, yes." She cleared her throat. "We give thanks to Samsin, the gods watching over Hana as she grows, and we pray for wealth, longevity and luck."

"Amen," Gina said.

Ian laughed and she apologized. "No, Meema," he said. "That's perfect."

Hana began to stir as they passed around the final plate, which contained small, baked items all crowded together. They were round with dark spots on top, like eyeballs.

"Take a couple," Ian instructed. "These are rice cakes. Families served these at the ceremony, and they sent out parcels to everyone they knew. Sometimes, people would send back the container with a ball of thread, to signify a long life."

"Yes, we still do this," Mrs. Kim said.

Gina thought of the image she'd had of her mother, floating amongst celestial bodies, trailing thread behind her. And somehow there was a comfort in it, as though the thread connected back to them, to Hana now.

As Ian was taking care of the bill with the manager, Carrie tapped Gina on the arm. "Can you hold her, please? I need to use the restroom."

And the world stopped spinning as Gina grabbed Hana under the arms and lifted her up, watched her wonderful brown eyes as they focused on her. The baby fit perfectly against her chest, her tiny face resting on the white sweater, her smooth skin cool and warm at the same time on Gina's neck.

"What a picture," Ian said.

She looked up through watery eyes to see her brother, his happy face and a drop of red sauce on his chin, watching the scene and looking, in that moment, completely full.

"I want to go to Namsan Tower," Ian announced.

They had finally left the restaurant, had buckled Hana back into the car seat and tucked the embroidered blanket around her legs. Carrie sat in the back, one arm draped across the baby. "Ian, no. It's been a long morning."

He looked at her in the rearview mirror. "Are you feeling okay?"

"Yes," she said, "but I was hoping to get back to the hotel—"

"Hear me out," he said. "It's only one o'clock and the sun is shining. The weather report calls for rain tomorrow morning and we won't have much time anyway, because the flight is at two."

"It's cold," she said. "I'm not sure it's a good idea."

"The wind," Gina added.

"We live in Chicago," Ian said. "Were you hoping to spare her from cold weather and wind?"

Carrie frowned. "No, but we just got her. I mean, it doesn't even feel real yet, does it?" She turned and looked through the back window, as if someone was following them.

Ian turned onto the main, busier road. "Who knows when we'll be back here, if ever. I've heard you can see the whole city from up there."

"How do you get to the top?" Gina asked.

He shrugged. "A cable car, then an elevator."

"I don't know," Carrie said.

"There's one baby and three of us." Ian raised an eyebrow. "I think we can manage. I had three people looking out for me and look how I turned out."

Gina had been watching the distant mountains, the haze that seemed to coat them like a layer of cotton. "Who?" she asked.

"Mom, you and Deborah."

"What about Dad?"

He shrugged. "I don't remember much about Dad, Meema."

She turned and looked again out the window. Cars sped by, their windows foggy, and exhales of smoke trailing behind. At the forks in the road, the exchanges where some merged into their path and others left it, Gina would watch a silver car, or a white one, wondering where they were headed. Like specters, the fogged-in drivers, the shadowy cars. Her grandmother, whose presence could be summoned with the scent of strong coffee or the lace trim of a bedspread, and her father—his gentleness, the ink-smudged fingertips—to Ian, these two were more concept than reality, faded and indistinct, vanishing. This fact was sad at times, at others, comforting. She was the link, and she was still here.

They parked the car where directed by an attendant and began to walk up a hill. Others were with them, a family of chattering blondes, a father and teenaged son, two young girls in high, colorful socks and short skirts. Ian held the baby against his chest in a cloth carrier, her legs splayed out to each side, the unmarred soles of her tiny shoes bouncing up and down.

It was damp and cold, but they warmed with the walk. They talked a bit at first but as the hill grew steeper, voices quieted. The young girls paused a few times to take photos of each other. Ian took the lead in their small, triangle formation, looking back occasionally to check on Carrie.

They came to the cable car area, where a small queue was formed. From here, they could see Namsan Tower, the white base and bulbous structure midway, the red and white spike rising from that. As they waited, Ian removed Hana from the carrier. A sweat-stained impression, baby-sized, darkened the front of his t-shirt. He zipped up his jacket. The transfer of the baby was a nerve-wracking, complicated maneuver. At times, when a leg missed the proper opening or the baby's head tilted unnaturally, Gina had to restrain herself from interfering. She had to trust they'd figure it out.

They huddled together in the cable car. People crowded in until Gina's shoulder rubbed against the father from the blonde family.

"Cozy," Ian said. "We'll be warm for the ride up."

Hana, who had slept during lunch and again briefly in the car, gazed around now with blinking eyes. Carrie had her faced outward and supported with her two hands over the carrier.

"Let her see through the window," Ian said.

Carrie wriggled until she was facing outside.

The doors closed and after an initial jerk, the cable car lifted smoothly. Gina sucked her breath in, watching the people, the trees, the buildings, all of it reducing to an incomprehensible size. The cable trailed behind them, secured to the earth.

"Look at that," Ian said.

They passed Namsan Mountain, a tree-covered, steep hill adjacent to the tower. Gina looked down at the plush, uninhabited greenness. They squeezed into another holding area, then an elevator. From the ground, the round viewing area looked like strips of metal wrapped around the tower. Once they stood outside, however, it was quite roomy. In the center, within the tower, was a restaurant and a shop and along one side of the concrete viewing deck, a metal fence crowded with padlocks.

"It's not too crowded," Carrie said. "Does she look cold?"

Ian shook his head. "You've got her fairly bundled up."

"I wish the sun would stay out," she said.

"I need to use the restroom," Gina said. "I'll be right back."

She had seen something in the shop, a surprise for Ian and Carrie. After she'd made her purchase, she found them along the rail, looking out over Seoul. It really was a beautiful view, the rolling land fitted with buildings, the black mountains framing everything, the blue and gray wisps of sky.

"I have something for you," she said. "For you and Carrie."

Ian turned around and took the paper bag from her outstretched hand. Reaching in, he removed the padlock, a silver one decorated with a red heart. A metal key protruded from the end.

"We don't have to do that." He glanced at Carrie.

"Oh," Gina said. "I thought—you told me about the custom."

Carrie stepped forward. With the baby's head under her chin and their black hair and brown eyes lined up, they reminded Gina of Russian nesting dolls that fit one inside the other, smaller and smaller.

"Thank you, Gina," she said. "What a special gift. Look, Ian, we can write something on the heart."

Gina handed over the stubbed pencil she'd gotten inside. She avoided looking at Ian, who apparently loved every ceremony known to man except the one she tried to help with.

"I'll write our names and the date." Carrie grabbed the lock from Ian and leaned forward to see over Hana's shoulder. She had a hard time balancing the lock and the pencil around the baby.

"Give it to me," Ian said. When he was done, he turned the lock to show them. He had written "Carrie is hot for Ian" with the date underneath. "Let's find a spot at the very top," he said.

"Never mind," Gina said. "Give it back."

"Ian," Carrie warned, but Gina could tell she was trying not to smile.

Gina reached out but he swiped the lock away. "Give it, Ian."

He dangled the lock over her head and despite her efforts to ignore the bait, she jumped and grabbed at it. Then she kicked his shin with her boot.

"You're a baby yourself," Carrie said to him, shaking her head.

He grabbed Gina around the shoulder and pulled her close. "Thanks, Meema. This is very thoughtful."

Stubbornly, she pulled away, shaking her head.

She watched as they walked to the row of padlocks and looked for a place to attach theirs. The young girls in the short skirts were posing as another tourist took a photo. Gina wandered to the long rail and took in the view. She wondered if one of the mountains was the same, flat-topped one she'd seen from the airplane. The city spread out and from this angle, afforded no clues. Up here, she lost her bearings, had no sense of where she was in the world. And it was liberating. As if her whole life was being reset, time and space changing everything.

Carrie approached and settled in next to Gina, shoulder to shoulder. "Ian's gone for a snack," she said, "then I think we should get going. We can rest for a while at the hotel and have dinner downstairs. We need to be up and packed early tomorrow. I want to allow extra time because of the luggage and of course, our new passenger. I'm going to give her a bath tonight. Oh, my God, I still can't believe this is happening. My parents are supposed to meet us at the airport. I can't wait for them to see her. Oh, Gina, I'm sorry."

"What?"

She smiled and leaned down to rub her lips against Hana's hair. "I'm rambling."

"I like it," Gina said. "Let's find Ian and head back. The baby's nose is red."

Carrie nodded and followed her inside. They found Ian talking to the father and son who'd walked with them to the cable car. Each of them held a candy bar, purchased in the shop behind them. When he saw the women, Ian grinned and waved them over. "Carrie, they're from St. Louis!" he announced, as if it was the most exciting thing in the world.

Gina glanced at her sister-in-law. "You have your hands full now, don't you?"

Carrie shrugged and gave her a firm push. "We both do."

22

Berwyn, January 2000

Gina shuffled into the kitchen in her slippers. A new pair, red with silk trim, quite fancy and exactly what she told Ian and Carrie to buy her for Christmas. She was almost sorry to discard the old blue ones, but the rubber sole had separated from the fabric on the left slipper and a hole had worn through over the big toe on the right. Nothing lasts forever, she told herself.

She set her mug of coffee on the wooden cabinet, which she had moved from one wall over to the space next to the window. The couch needed to be shifted a bit to accommodate it, but she liked the new symmetry of the room, the way her belongings had been rearranged for the featured item: a portable crib for Hana. A "pack and play" Carrie called it, and she showed Gina how it could be folded up and stored. Pale green with tiny pink dots, a thin mattress and white netting for walls. Hana's stuffed koi fish was propped in the corner. Gina preferred to keep the crib set up all the time, in case they ever stopped by unannounced, in case they needed her on short notice.

On the top shelf in the cabinet was a small stack of CDs. Five, to be exact. Three discs Ian and Carrie had given her with the CD player that, along with the slippers, had been her Christmas presents. Two of them by someone named Raffi—melodic, catchy tunes she'd find herself humming for days afterwards—and another by four brightly-shirted men called The Wiggles. That one was Gina's least favorite, but Hana seemed to prefer it. She perked up whenever it came on, clapping her hands and searching for the radio, as if expecting to see them there. Carrie explained that The Wiggles also had a television show Hana watched, the only one sure to keep her attention. She was fourteen months old.

Gina glanced at the VHS tapes on the bottom shelf. Extinct, Ian said of them. Gina still had a VCR in the living room, but he said she'd be hard pressed to have it repaired and it would be nearly impossible to find another one within a few years. Everything was on disc now. She grabbed the CD she wanted, a compilation of Elvis Presley songs, pushed the button on the player and nestled the disc inside. *Blue Christmas* was number three.

First the chorus of high voices in the background, then Elvis's croon coming in, a distinctive overlay, the first verse of *Blue Christmas*.

Gina had kept the spiral notebooks, the many letters to her imagined daughter, hidden behind the row of VHS tapes where she could only catch an occasional glimpse, to remind her of the distraction they'd provided for so long. Telling Mrs. Spark hadn't been as difficult as she'd imagined. The old woman had shown uncharacteristic restraint. She listened as Gina explained that she had wanted something, someone, to talk about, and the fabrication had leapt from her mouth before it was even a tangible idea. Afterwards, she said, it was like making up a story, filling in details and events. Something to do.

Mrs. Spark had clamped her mouth shut, lifting the teacup to her lips now and again, watching with cautious but caring eyes. After Gina finished, she folded her hands on the placemat and said, "I have to tell you, Gina. I've lived seventy-nine years. I've heard things that would make your head spin. I've seen things I don't care to talk about." She lifted the lid of the sugar jar and put it in its place. "So, you don't have a daughter after all. Big deal."

And she began to understand that Mrs. Spark was going to excuse her, without any stipulations. Across the table, her old eyes twinkled.

"I'm sorry," Gina said.

Mrs. Spark raised her bony hand as if shooing a fly. "I tell you I have a son, but sometimes it doesn't feel that way."

Gina saw her elderly neighbor in a new light after that day. She realized if you lived long enough, you're able to prioritize and see what's important. Hopefully.

She closed the cupboard door and went to the portable crib, where she straightened the baby blanket draped over its side. Elvis continued his song, almost a mantra now, the same lyrics repeated over and over, the vision of blue snowflakes, red decorations on a green tree, all of it rushing in.

They'd had a wonderful holiday, the best she could remember since the exciting ones when she was a child. She'd always wake up first, then get Deborah. Together, they'd creep down the stairs and stare with their mouths gaping at the mound of gifts. In later years, when they were older and the holiday was beginning to lose some of its magic, Ian had rekindled it. He took over the role of family alarm clock, climbing onto Gina's bed with his cold feet, jumping around her slumbering body until she agreed to go with him downstairs. Then they'd go back up for their parents. Usually, their mother was already awake, her keen hearing having alerted her. They'd shake their father's shoulder and laugh at the startled, sleepy expression on his face when he opened his eyes.

This past Christmas had rivaled those. Ian and Carrie invited her to spend Christmas Eve at their loft so she could be there in the morning to see the look on Hana's face when she discovered her own mound of gifts. There was a plastic grocery cart she could eventually push around, and bags of pretend food. There were stuffed animals and soft cloth books, building blocks and a doll with brown yarn hair. They had Chinese food for dinner, ordered in from one of the few restaurants open for business, and Gina drove home after that.

Sometimes she went downtown to visit them. Usually, she had no problem finding a parking space near their building. She liked their neighborhood more now. A small grocer had opened a store on the corner and two of the condos on their floor were occupied. Ian and Carrie had become friendly with the young couple next door and another neighbor, a kind, older gentleman who assured them he never heard the baby through the thick walls. On Christmas day, they used the fireplace, which burned gas instead of logs but kept the entire place cozy. After she opened her red slippers, Gina wore them all day and sometimes, she even felt a little too warm.

She crossed the room and pulled open the curtains to let the sun in. Across the short distance, she could see that Mrs. Spark had forgotten to turn off the patio decoration lights again. She was constantly reminding the old woman. Some of the ornaments were ancient, all of them exposed to the elements constantly. Gina worried about an electrical fire. But Mrs. Spark was stubborn and forgetful and when one of these traits lessened momentarily, the other amplified.

In the kitchen, the telephone rang. Gina glanced at the time. Ian and Carrie should be on their way but recently, Ian had started carrying around a cellular phone and using it with great frivolity. She crossed the room and picked up the receiver. She couldn't really see the purpose of having a telephone with you all the time.

"Hello, Ian," she said.

"Uh, Gina?" An unfamiliar voice. Not Ian.

"Yes, sorry. This is Gina."

"Hey there, it's Paul."

She steadied herself against the counter. "Paul."

"How are you?"

"Good."

"It's been a while," he said.

"Yes," she said. "Was it October?"

"Sure was."

"Paul, could you hold on a second?"

"Okay."

Carefully, Gina set the receiver on the counter and padded over to the port-a-crib. The stuffed koi fish stared with its purple eyes; the blanket was still folded over the side.

She remembered the dinner at Nehra's, her embarrassing fall, and the visit from Paul afterwards. Everything else had avalanched after that night. The trip to Korea. Ian and Carrie. Hana. In quiet moments, images returned to her: Paul's green eyes across the table, his arms crossed on her back, her legs relaxing on the couch. But she'd been so busy. She spoke to Ian and Carrie almost every day to see how everyone was doing. They'd heard stories about wailing babies, culture-shocked and jet-lagged, breaking down the resolves of new parents in a matter of days. But Hana was an angel. She'd adapted easily to a feeding schedule and rarely had a problem falling asleep. Gina hadn't known many babies, but Hana had a sweet temperament and was so smart. It was impossible to imagine things any other way. It was as though she'd always been with them.

Thoughts of Paul were rare in those first weeks back from Korea. Gina dominated conversations at work, talking about which new food Carrie had mashed up in the food processor, how Hana had reacted to a gift toy, what Ian had said about child-rearing. When Nehra invited her for dinner over Memorial Day weekend, Gina stalled, not ready to face her friend's home again, especially with the same cast of characters. Instead, she agreed to meet at a restaurant closer to Berwyn.

Seeing Paul again wasn't as awkward as she'd imagined, and the foursome enjoyed a new Italian restaurant. Gina controlled her wine intake that night and they talked about movies and gardening, about work and the city. Once, it seemed that Paul's foot had brushed hers the circular table. She scooted closer to Nehra then convinced herself she'd imagined it.

She never asked Paul for his telephone number, and he never asked for hers. They met up again over the summer, again at Nehra and Tom's, again for a meal that was perfectly pleasant. Tom barbecued bratwurst and chicken, and Nehra made a vegetable dish with squash and tomatoes from Paul's garden. They sat outside on the patio furniture and drank sangria in moderation.

At work, Nehra began to get pushy. She seemed to view it as a personal failure that Gina and Paul hadn't galloped off into the sunset or at least, made arrangements to see each other without her intervention. Her last, most intense effort had been in early October. She arranged for Paul to pick up Gina and meet her and Tom at the farmer's market. They'd shop a bit and have lunch at one of the food stands at the outskirts of the market. Nehra made it clear that they had plans later in the afternoon, but Gina and Paul should feel free to stay for an afternoon concert planned at the park across the street. Jazz violinists, she said. Gershwin and other classics. Something she was certain they'd like.

And the strange thing about it, as Gina thought back to that day, was they *had* liked it. After lunch, they sat on the blanket Paul had thoughtfully packed, sipping their strawberry lemonades and tapping their feet to the music. They talked about Paul's parents, who weren't getting any younger, and about Hana, whose world widened at every turn. They laughed and enjoyed the music. Then Paul drove her home, where they shared a very pleasant goodbye. She hadn't spoken to him since.

Gina walked back to the kitchen and lifted the telephone receiver. "Paul?"

"There you are." He sounded relieved, or impatient. She couldn't be sure.

"I had to check on something," she told him. "Hana's coming today."

"How is she?"

"Fourteen months old now. She's getting ready to walk."

"They're sweet, aren't they?"

"I don't know about other babies," she said. "But this one is."

"My mom used to say babies are always more trouble than you expect and much more wonderful." He chuckled. "I don't remember her having much patience with six of us running around, but she's always loved babies."

"Nehra told me your mother was ill," Gina said. "I should have called."

"No, it's all right." He shuffled the receiver. "She's much better now, back home. Lorraine keeps an eye out. They're all in La Grange still. I've been spending a lot of my free time down there."

"That's good."

"Hey, listen." He paused and Gina could feel her heart thumping, up near her throat. "I was wondering if you'd like to catch a movie sometime, maybe have dinner?"

"I could do that," she said. "I mean, I'd like to."

"The two of us."

"Oh," she said.

"I know it's been a while. I don't know what I've been waiting for." He cleared his throat. "You'd think I'd have a better read on women with all these sisters but to be honest, Gina, I never could tell if you'd invite it. Me calling, I mean. But I should have. I should've gone with my gut, or my heart, or whatever."

"It's fine," she said.

"You get set in your ways," he said. "Didn't we talk about that? The first night? The older you get, you're bogged down with these habits." He chuckled. "Every time you turn around, there you are, getting in your own way."

"Paul." She pressed her hand to her cheek. "Dinner would be nice."

"Gina, I want to be clear. I have a good time with you and that would be all right, wouldn't it? Dinner once in a while, or a movie? I know you like your movies."

She narrowed her eyes. "What's wrong with movies?"

"Not a damn thing."

She smiled. "It's nice to hear from you."

He cleared his throat. "How about next Saturday? And dinner—don't forget a meal is included. That isn't the weekend you're going to Galena?"

Her mind worked. How did he know about her planned trip with Nehra? "No, that's next month. Her nephew's wedding."

"I ran into Tom last week," he explained. "Came down to work with his brother. I called later that night to ask for your telephone number. I hadn't seen them, either, not since we all went to the farmer's market."

She looked out the window at the gray expanse above Mrs. Spark's condo. "Remember how sunny and warm it was?" she asked. "Not like October at all."

"You remember?" he said.

"Of course." She straightened her back, pressed the telephone closer to her ear. "I'd better get going."

"Six o'clock?" he asked. "I'll pick you up."

"Sure."

"Where do you want to eat?"

"You decide," she said. "Surprise me."

"At least look at the movie listings, if that's what you want to do."

"I will."

"Goodbye, Gina."

"Bye."

She hung up and hurried down the hall. Her face was warm against the cool air in the hallway. She wondered if she should adjust the heat for the baby. The phone call had set her back a bit. She'd have to finish her coffee between the steps of her morning bathroom routine. She pulled open a drawer in her dresser and found the velour pants and zipped hoodie, and a colored tee-shirt to go underneath. She liked to wear stretchy clothes so she could easily get on the floor and play with Hana.

She wasn't sure how to feel about Paul's phone call or the date they'd made. He was right, she did enjoy movies, and who didn't like eating out? And she'd meant it when she said she enjoyed his company. Wasn't that enough, at least for now? She felt a pleasant buzz.

Years of practice had ensured she could get through her toiletries quickly if necessary. She was showered, with dry hair and lipstick applied, and listening to the Elvis collection for the second time when Ian and Carrie arrived.

She heard their car as it pulled off the main road, then Ian's knock crackled through the empty condo. They came in and settled their things: a bright, patterned diaper bag and another paper bag with snacks and bottles, a third canvas bag with toys and books.

When he noticed the music playing, Ian asked, "What's this?"

"It's Elvis," she said. "The king."

He raised his eyebrows. "You're developing some strange habits."

"What do you mean? You bought the CD player for me. What am I supposed to do with it?"

"I never knew you liked Elvis."

"He's fantastically musical," she said, bending to lift Hana.

The top of the baby's hair was pulled into a ponytail, the black tips spilling over like water from a fountain. She babbled continuously, unable to pull her attention from the rubber item in her little hands. She stared at it, chewed it, then brought it away from her face to study it.

"What's that?" Gina asked.

"It's a dreidel," Carrie said. "For Hanukkah. You remember our neighbors, Candice and Jay? They gave it to her."

"Oh," she said.

"It's a baby version, of course. Usually they're wooden."

Ian came forward and wiped a bit of drool from Hana's mouth with a white cloth. "We're equal opportunity parents in the religion department."

Carrie usually packed at least twenty of the cloths in the bag whenever Hana stayed with Gina. They apparently never wanted the baby to have anything on her, ever.

"I'm going to run into the bathroom before we go," Carrie said. "Lately, I feel like I'm in there all the time. Probably too much tea this morning."

"Go ahead," Gina said. When they heard Carrie shut the door, she gave Ian an inquisitive look.

"What?"

"You don't have anything to tell me? Any reason she might be using the bathroom a lot?"

He stared at her, blankly.

She shrugged. "Never mind."

"Look at this, Hana," he said. "Your Auntie Meema has everything set up for you."

"I've got locks on the kitchen cupboards since the last time she was here," Gina said. "And I bought that gate. I can close off the hallway and she can crawl around in here."

"Perfect," Ian said.

"Do you mind if I take her over to see Mrs. Spark? She looks forward to it, you know. And Hana loves looking at all that stuff on the porch. You should see the way she stares. Wants to touch everything, but I'll hold her because I don't know how safe any of that wiring is. I keep telling Mrs. Spark to take some of it down, but she ignores me." Gina put Hana in the pack and play, along with a few toys she found in one of the bags. "she told me her grandkids used to love that stuff. Her son brought them more often when they were young." She shook her head. "I feel sorry for her. Now that they've moved to Texas, I'm not sure she'll ever see them. He barely gave her the time of day when he was nearby."

"That's too bad. Does she still have that shirt?"

"What, the *I've Got Seoul* tee-shirt?"

Ian smiled.

"She wears it every time Hana's here," she said.

"You should definitely take her over." He sat on the couch, his belly making the shirt extend a bit over his belt.

For some time, after they had returned from Korea and settled back into their lives, Ian had lost quite a bit of weight. Throughout the warmer months, he took Hana for long walks around the city. He seemed to really enjoy it, Carrie said, pushing the stroller down the sidewalks, being asked about her. He was so proud. Lately, he seemed to have gained some back.

"I talked to Deborah the other day," Gina said.

"So did I," Ian said. "She must have been making the rounds."

She looked up, trying to read his tone.

He shrugged. "At least I'm in the rounds now."

"She might come this summer," Gina said. "Bring the boys and Dan."

"Where would they stay?"

"Downtown probably. A hotel. I'll drive down," she said.

Ian nodded. He had shaved his beard, finally. She remembered the beginning of it, when they were in Seoul. Carrie kept the embroidered blanket, the gift from the Korean foster mother, in Hana's crib at home. Eventually, she planned to cut out a section from the design and frame it.

"Deborah's very interested in your trip to Galena," Ian said.

"She's not the only one."

"What?"

"Oh, nothing."

Ian put his hands behind his head and leaned back on the couch. "She told me to make sure you buy a dress that shows your legs. I had to remind her that I am your brother and not another sister, and that this would not be an appropriate topic."

"But you're bringing it up now."

"Yes, I am." His eyes twinkled. "I wanted to see your reaction."

"It's no surprise, if that's what you mean. She told me the same thing herself."

"About the legs?"

"Yes," she said, refusing to meet his eyes.

"Whose legs?" Carrie said as she returned.

"Deborah thinks Meema should show her legs at that wedding."

Carrie turned towards her. "You do have nice legs."

Gina flushed. "When are you two leaving?"

Ian laughed and stood up. "We're going to have lunch and go to a matinee. It'll probably be four, four-thirty when we get back. Is that okay?"

"Of course," she said. "You could leave her until Tuesday for all I care."

"Be careful what you ask for," Carrie said. "She had a short nap on the way here. She may go back down but she may not. Sorry."

"It's fine. Have a good time. Don't worry about anything." Gina felt, for a moment, that she might cry, so thankful was she for their trust. They had left Hana with her many times now, usually some weekend afternoon for shopping or a movie, and on a few occasions, she'd watched the baby at their place. Ian didn't want Hana to ride with Gina in her car; it was unspoken but understood. And she didn't mind. Gina realized she wasn't the best driver, and they all had to put Hana's well-being over any other considerations. She hadn't even minded when Ian told her they expected her to abstain from cocktails whenever she had the baby. Of course, she only had the one drink, a few times a week and usually, long after dinner, but she hadn't minded the topic being raised. She had known Ian would be a responsible father. The first time she babysat, he told her, "None of us are child development experts like your Mr. Seutter. We'll figure this out together."

When they left, Gina locked the door. The sun was glaring through the window now, so she blocked it a little with the curtain. The lighting was perfect after that. She checked the thermostat, which she had set much warmer than she would if she were in the condo alone. She walked over to the pack and play, reached in and felt Hana's tiny hand, making sure it wasn't cold. Hana pulled herself to a standing position. She lifted her arms and clenched and unclenched her fists while making an *uh* sound. It was the way she said, "Pick me up."

Hana wasn't walking yet, and Carrie was tired of people asking about it. "She'll walk when she walks," she always said. Gina knew it wouldn't be long. Hana was steady on her feet. She could walk the length of the room if she had something to hold onto; she could push her little grocery cart for several steps. She didn't believe yet that she could do it unassisted. But she would.

For Hana's first birthday in November, Carrie and Ian held a party at a Korean restaurant on Clark Street. After they enjoyed traditional food, a man in a white robe came to deliver a special blessing. He set a variety of items on the table. The idea was that Hana would choose one to represent her future career. Ian guided the baby around the table, and she chose, among the many items, a book. Gina suspected her brother had coached Hana, but she could never prove it.

Gina lifted her niece onto her hip and kissed her warm cheek. The baby looked at her sideways, nestled her face into the side of Gina's neck, then leaned back again. Although it was impossible, in that moment she looked exactly like Ian, the dark hair, the bright, inquisitive eyes.

"Let's take a look around," Gina said. "There's so many things to show you." It was a favorite game, walking around the condo, naming items. She pointed out the Firecracker Flower, which had rallied and survived, currently without blooms but the leaves were green and moist. Gina showed her the green lamps, the glasses in the cupboard, the food in the refrigerator, naming each item as she went along and watching with delight when something caught the baby's interest. And when they both tired of the game and Hana began to get a little cranky, Gina heated up a bottle and settled her onto the tiny mattress. She knew from experience that Hana didn't like to be held as she fell asleep. Maybe it was something retained from her time in the foster home or those few days in the agency; maybe it was something particular about her personality. A certain independence.

Gina turned down the volume on the CD player and started the music again. In a little while, she would get up and make a cup of tea. When Hana woke up, they'd head over to Mrs. Spark's, maybe invite the old woman back for a while. Tomorrow would be another busy day at the office. Mr. Seutter was working on a new project and there was much to do. Next Saturday, she'd have dinner with Paul.

Settling into the chair next to the crib, Gina kicked off her slippers. She picked up the stuffed koi fish and hugged it against her chest. She breathed, listening to the steady tick of the living room clock. In time, the ticks seemed to synchronize with the beat of her stubborn heart, and with the turning of the wide, wide earth itself. She thought about her parents, her mother's styled hair and beige, high-waist slacks, and his hands, pale and smooth, and the crevice between his eyebrows. The feel of them, the ways they loved her. She wondered what they would think of this granddaughter from across the world. Would her father hold Hana on his lap, showing her photos of the blue and purple electrical pathways? Would her mother carry the baby around, pointing out the curtains with their blue gondolas, the reaching trees outside the window on Euclid Street, the staircase with its worn center?

Gina put her feet up and closed her eyes, listening to the holiday music and feeling the full effect of the day, and the possibility of those to follow, while she waited for the sounds of Hana's dreaming.

ABOUT THE AUTHOR

Mary Vensel White is the author of the novels *Bellflower* and *The Qualities of Wood*. Her short fiction and essays have appeared in numerous publications. She is an English and writing professor and owner of *Type Eighteen Editing* Services. Born in Los Angeles, she attended college in Denver and Chicago and has been back in California for over twenty years. She still considers Chicago a second hometown and visits often.

CPSIA information can be obtained
at www.ICGtesting.com
Printed in the USA
BVHW041511120522
PP13536200001B/5/J